THE HANDBOOK FOR WORKING SINGERS

THE HANDBOOK FOR WORKING SINGERS

ROMA WATERMAN

**SCHIRMER
TRADE BOOKS**
part of The Music Sales Group

Exclusive Distributors
Music Sales Limited,
8/9 Frith Street,
London W1D 3JB, UK.

Music Sales Corporation,
257 Park Avenue South,
New York, NY 10010, USA.

Macmillan Distribution Services,
53 Park West Drive,
Derrimut, Vic 3030,
Australia.

To the Music Trade only:
Music Sales Limited,
8/9 Frith Street,
London W1D 3JB, UK.

Every effort has been made to trace the copyright holders of the photographs in this
book but one or two were unreachable. We would be grateful if the photographers
concerned would contact us.

Printed by: Gutenberg Press Ltd., Malta

A catalogue record for this book is available from the British Library.

www.musicsales.com

Contents

Part II Performance

Part III Maintenance

Foreword

It was in 1998 that I received a telephone call from a young lady with a very husky speaking voice. She had been diagnosed with a nodule on the vocal fold, a problem that is all too common with contemporary singers. The so-called 'industry' is a minefield for poorly trained or untrained singers who have to contend with many living and working conditions that are far from ideal for the human singing voice. This was how Roma Waterman came into my life.

A vibrant, enthusiastic singer and composer, Roma was in serious trouble with her voice. In such a situation there is no half way. Old patterns have to be replaced with new ones, and this takes much hard work (on the part of both singer and teacher), as well as a great deal of courage, determination, time, and patience. Roma applied herself with a singleness of purpose and, within six months, her nodule had disappeared. She had gained an understanding of her voice and she was free to interpret her own compositions.

When Roma approached me to act as consultant/advisor for this handbook, I did have some reservations. There are many books on the market about singing—some good and some, well, … ? It has been impossible not to be caught up with the fresh approach and directness of Roma's work, and the overall approach of her book. She has produced a workable, practical, and valuable handbook which should be a very useful quick reference for singers—whatever the area in which they perform.

On all counts Roma Waterman—'Brava!'

Loris Synan
Melbourne, Australia
2002

Loris Synan

Loris Synan, distinguished performer, teacher, and adjudicator, teaches singing at the Faculty of Music, Victorian College of the Arts, University of Melbourne. In 1996, she was granted a Churchill Fellowship to study methods of breathing in Europe. These have proven to be of great value to professional voice users and people suffering from voice problems through excessive tension. She was the first Australian to be invited to join the prestigious Cooegium of Medicorum et Teatri (CoMeT), and is the keynote speaker for the International Voice Conference in New Zealand, 2003.

About the author

Roma Waterman is a professional singer and songwriter who resides in Melbourne, Australia. Growing up in an Italian family, Roma was encouraged in her love for music, and was blessed with singing and piano lessons throughout her younger years (although, in the early days, these were by force!).

Roma has worked as a session singer on numerous live and studio recordings, and also runs the Melbourne Gospel Choir which performs regularly on television. She has worked with many Australian artists including Vanessa Amorossi, Jay La'Gaia, Julie Anthony, Debra Byrne, and Marina Prior, and with international artists such as Reba McIntrye and DC Talk.

Roma's wide experience has equipped her well to teach singing to many professional and semi-professional performers. She runs many lectures on vocal technique, and also has the pleasure of being a member of the House 2 House Band with many other talented musicians.

Roma's passion is for her original material, and she has produced several albums which have sold extremely well in Australia and overseas. Over the past ten years or so this has led to extensive touring, and a publishing deal with Warner Chappell music.

For more information on Roma Waterman you can check out her website at <www.romawaterman.com>.

Acknowledgments

Writing and publishing a book is no easy job! There are so many people I want to acknowledge and thank for helping me get this book out.

I especially want to thank Loris Synan—my wonderful singing teacher, and the consultant and advisor for this book. I certainly could not have done this without you! I appreciate all the time you have put into me and this project. You have helped me to create a work that I can be proud of.

I also want to express my gratitude to all the wonderful people who gave their time and efforts to help make this book possible. I appreciate all of you giving your time and talents. So thanks to; Terry Martinesz (Personal Nutrition Services); Phil Butson (Sing Sing Studios); Angelo DiPietro (naturopath); Andrew Naylor; Justin Douglas (Ebony Recording Studios); Robert J. Powell; Janine Maunder; Esther Oakley; Andrew Gorrie; Rebecca Watkins; Ross Gilham; Josephine Abbatangelo; Brendan Imer; Melbourne Eye and Ear Hospital; Rebecca Davies; Steve Filby; Amanda Blanchard-Sell; Derek Bailey and Zara Antony.

Thanks also to everyone at Christian City Church, Whitehorse, Australia, for your advice and friendship. If it's true that you are only as great as the people around you, then I truly have a lot of greatness within me!

Also special thanks to my mum and dad, Rosalie and Don Balassone, and Nola Waterman, for unending belief in any project I set my hand to. If I do well in life, it is because I have great role models like you.

Last but not least, I want to thank my wonderful husband, Ted Waterman, who never ceases to believe in me. Being around you has made me a better person, and I love you muchly (more than ice-cream, in fact!).

Roma Waterman
Melbourne, Australia
2002

Introduction

Introduction
Me, myself, and I—a three-piece

Welcome!

Well Hi! I'm so glad you've picked up my book. If you've been singing for a while you might have noticed that there are lots of books and various techniques for singers. So let me give you the facts up front. I am *not* a famous speech therapist. I am *not* a leading laryngologist. I have *not* invented some amazing new technique. I am a singer—just like you. This is why I think this book can be of help to you.

I'm a singer who has experienced vocal difficulties in the past, and who has spent most of my years learning how to rectify them. I have been where you are and experienced problems just like you. And I have found out what works and what does not work. I am hoping that this book appeals to you because I am writing about what I have lived through and put into practice for myself.

I believe that this book is a good start for you, and I believe that this book can be a useful reference manual for you for many years to come. It will help you to understand how your voice works, and how to get the best out of it—from someone who has lived it, and not just read about it.

I know from first-hand experience that the stuff in this book works. It is not a new technique or a secret method for getting the best out of your voice. Rather, it is 'down-to-earth' advice that I hope will always be a help to you in your career as a working singer. I have really enjoyed writing it, and I look forward to helping you as much as I can!

In the beginning ...

I thought you might want to know a bit about my journey up to this point. If you don't—well, you can just skip this part!

I can't remember a time when I didn't want to sing. I'm sure there are many of you who feel that way as well. I spent most of my childhood years having piano and singing lessons, sitting for the Australian Music Examinations Board (AMEB) music exams at the Victorian College of the Arts, singing in choirs, eisteddfods, churches, old people's homes, and so on. I couldn't get enough of singing! I would even put on concerts at home for my family and force my brothers and sisters to be part of a 'concert extravaganza'! The kitchen chairs were the front-row seats, and the lounge-room doors were the stage curtains.

Coming from an Italian family, there was music all the time. My uncle and grandfather played the piano accordion, and it was my uncle who initially taught me to play the piano. (I hope I *never* have to play 'Green Sleeves' again!) I grew up in church, which was a great arena in which to improve as a musician, and as a person. It meant I was singing every weekend to people who loved me and who encouraged my craft.

I have always loved to write songs and I often dreamt of the day when I could be a full-time musician and release my own albums. I was the ultimate daydreamer.

I left school after Year 12, and all my years of classical training paid off— I started a full-time job as a secretary! I continued to do music on the side, hoping that one day I would be able to fulfil my life-long dream.

After a couple of years, I took the jump and began working in music full time. It was both exciting and scary. I did a bit of session work and began to perform my own original material. It wasn't long before I decided to record my first album and see what happened.

My first record deal

I was given a distribution contract with a small Australian company and began to tour the country. It was all pretty exciting and I was privileged to tour as support for a lot of international artists such as DC Talk, Newsboys, Margaret Becker, David Meece, and Kenny Marks. It was a great privilege for me to tour with them. I saw how they lived and worked, and I learnt a lot about the music industry.

It wasn't long before I began to establish myself as an original artist. I was constantly touring and recording, and I found it difficult to keep up with the workload. I was not earning a lot of money (like most original artists), but I was working all the time and loved what I was doing. Life consisted of sleeping on people's floors, eating McDonald's for breakfast, lunch, and dinner, long hours in a tour bus, loud music, smoke machines, lots of laughing, and living on adrenalin and coffee. I loved it!

Amid all this I recorded a second album, went to the USA for some gigs and meetings, and was about to embark on another national tour when I started to feel a little ill.

The wake-up call

Because life was in the fast lane all the time, I didn't really pay attention when I was not feeling a hundred per cent. I was feeling pretty tired, my voice was feeling a little tight, and I had almost passed out a few times. When I fainted in the shower one cold morning in Sydney, I thought I had the 'flu.

Before I left home for a national tour I went to see a voice specialist. The doctor found a nodule forming on my right vocal fold and told me that I needed a three-month holiday. I was shocked! Despite all the training I had received, and all the knowledge I had gained, here I was—experiencing vocal difficulty. I was also told that I had glandular fever—and I didn't even know! I couldn't cancel my tour, which made the whole situation worse. I kept thinking about all the money the promoters would lose, and all the people I would be letting down.

As you are reading this, you can probably see all the things that led to this unfortunate situation. But, at the time, my hectic schedule was 'just life'. I had no idea that I was overdoing things. Needless to say, I should have listened to the doctor—but I didn't. I went on the tour as scheduled. I ended up passing out in the middle of a concert, being forced to fly home, and having to cancel the rest of the tour. The whole thing was a disaster!

Reassessing my values

I hated music. I hated singing. I was exhausted. Staying at home, buying a house, and having babies all began to seem very appealing to me! (As if that wouldn't be just as hard eh?)

I realised that I must reassess my values and what I wanted out of life. If I wanted to sing for the rest of my life, I had to start looking after myself. This crisis wasn't just about putting on a good show, or writing great songs, or just getting by vocally for a concert or two. It was about preserving my voice for the long haul.

So I went back to singing lessons with Loris Synan, and she saved my life! Loris worked me through voice therapy and disciplined me to continue studying for my classical exams. She taught me how to look after my voice and to *know* my voice—how to be in control, and to recognise the danger signals.

Things begin to look up!

Within a few months my nodule was gone. I continued my lessons after that, and I have had no problems since. I have become a lot more disciplined in taking care of my voice—on and off the road.

After a while, friends in the industry started coming to me for advice on how to look after their voices. Without setting out to become a vocal teacher or advisor, by default I began teaching people what I knew. It wasn't long before I was asked to speak at music conferences on vocal technique. I was quite surprised to discover that, like me, a lot of professional singers didn't know how their voices worked or how to look after them. Now I really enjoy helping my friends and colleagues know and care for their voices, as I continue to work and pursue my own music interests. A lot of dreams have come true for me, and I doubt if this would have happened had I not learnt to take care of my voice on a daily basis.

The biggest lesson I have learnt is that it doesn't matter how much you know—it will not make any difference if you don't put it into practice! With all my years of training, I still did not understand the basic principle of discipline. I still get it wrong sometimes, but I have committed myself to keep learning.

So the reason for this book is to help you learn. It is here as a tool for you, and for your voice. Take your time reading it—experiment, review, and, most importantly, enjoy!

PART 1
FOUNDATION

Chapter 1

How it all works—the physiology of the voice

Chapter 1
How it all works—the physiology of the voice

What is the best technique for my voice?

First and foremost, it's important to understand what is actually happening when you sing. Once you understand the mechanics of how your voice is produced, you will find it much easier to look after it and sing without tenseness.

There are many singing techniques, and there are many teachers who teach voice production without really understanding the physiology of the voice. I know several people who have had years of training who have not known how to sing a note without forcing their tone and putting pressure on their vocal folds. There are many teachers and students who *sound* great when they sing—but there is a difference between natural ability and good technique. Whether you sing classical, gospel, pop, or whatever, there are really only two ways to sing—the right way and the wrong way!

You will find it doesn't matter *what* you sing – it's *how* that's important. This is why it is imperative that you, as a singer, understand how it all works, so that no matter what style of music you are singing, you are doing it properly.

So let's look at what is actually happening to your voice and body when you sing.

Anatomy of head and throat

Have a look at Figure 1.1 (page 14). This shows the important structures of the head and throat that are involved in phonation (talking, singing, and so on). We will talk about each of the main structures involved——but without getting too technical! Although the vocal folds are the most important structures in phonation, it is easier to understand the anatomy if we work our way down from the top first.

Nasal cavity, nasal pharynx, soft palate, and oral pharynx

The pharynx is the space in the back of the mouth and nose, above the throat (see Figure 1.1). It is part of the vocal tract. The pharynx (oral and nasal), together with the soft palate and nasal cavity, are all used simultaneously to enhance the sound, colour, and amplification of your voice (which is basically produced in the vocal folds, see below). Tone should be free to resonate in the oral and nasal pharynx, the nasal cavity, and the mouth simultaneously. We will discuss these areas more in the chapter on resonance and vibration (see Chapter 4, page 45).

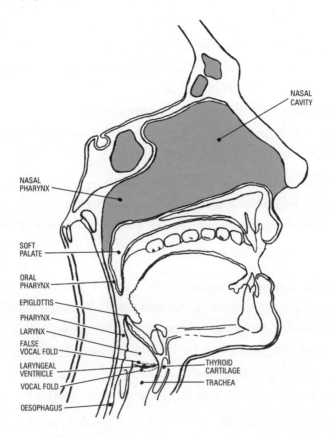

Figure 1.1

Head and neck structures important in singing

PUBLISHED WITH PERMISSION OF JOSEPHINE ABBATANGELO

Tongue and mouth

The shape of the soft palate and tongue create vowels. The lips, teeth, and tongue create consonants. Tenseness in the mouth can cause distortion and restriction of good tone, and part of vocal training should include exercises to relax the lower jaw. Some singers sing with their tongues 'hunched' up—which makes less space for the voice to move freely out of the mouth. Rigidity in the root of the tongue also causes considerable problems. Good vocal training is needed to rectify this problem.

Tension vs tenseness

A rule I follow when I am singing is that it should feel comfortable. Of course, there must be some *tension* in your body as you prepare to sing, but no *tenseness*—there is a difference.

If I am going for a long drive, I don't slump into the driver's seat ready to relax completely. Rather, I am alert, my mind is active, and I sit straight. But I am comfortable. There is a certain *tension*, but I am not experiencing *tenseness*.

It should be the same with singing.

Epiglottis

At the top of the trachea, above the larynx, sits the epiglottis (see Figure 1.1). When you swallow, the epiglottis closes over the trachea to prevent food and drink from entering the lungs. When it does not perform this function efficiently food can be caught in the trachea and you experience the uncomfortable feeling of choking.

Larynx

The larynx is right where your 'Adam's apple' is situated. It sits on top of your trachea or 'windpipe' (see Figure 1.1). The larynx is basically made up of cartilage (like soft bone), and the vocal folds are inside the larynx structure.

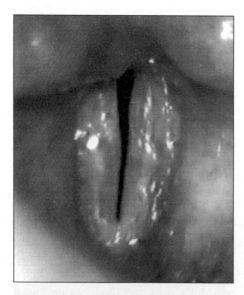

Figure 1.2
Vocal folds during phonation
(talking, screaming, or singing)
PUBLISHED WITH PERMISSION OF LUCY HOLMES

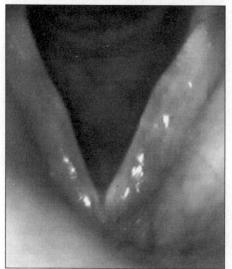

Figure 1.3
Vocal folds during rest and quiet breathing
PUBLISHED WITH PERMISSION OF LUCY HOLMES

Vocal folds

You can see where the vocal folds are (from the side) by looking at Figure 1.1. A close-up view of the vocal folds (from above) can be seen in Figures 1.2 and 1.3 (page 16). Your vocal folds lie in the centre of your larynx, and are long smoothly rounded bands of muscle and fibrous tissue. If you view them from above, these two folds look like a V, with small muscles surrounding the rear (or bottom) of the V.

When you sing or speak, air passes up through your windpipe and out through the vocal folds. This causes them to vibrate (very much like a wind or reed instrument) and produce sound. The frequency of vibration is about a hundred times per second—which is faster than the human eye can see.

When you take a deep breath, the vocal folds separate. When you are producing a sound, the vocal folds meet. This action, and the resulting sound, is called *phonation*.

False vocal folds

The false vocal folds are situated above the true vocal folds, and run parallel to them (see Figure 1.1). They help to protect the lower part of the larynx and the vocal folds. They do not produce sound.

Trachea

The trachea is also called the windpipe. When we sing or speak, air passes up through the windpipe and through the vocal folds, causing them to vibrate.

So all you need to do is breathe!

As you can see, your voice is produced by breath passing through your vocal folds—so it is very important that your breathing is working efficiently. If it isn't, you will find the muscles around your larynx doing more work than is necessary. You will tend to 'push' your notes out (especially if you are trying to increase volume), and you will experience throat tenseness. This can cause your voice to sound thin, 'reedy', rough, and 'breathy'.

Even if you have been singing incorrectly for a long time, you might not notice any discomfort. But remember—just because it doesn't hurt, this does not necessarily mean that there is no problem. You have to learn to read the signs that your body tells you. Are you breathing correctly? Are you singing with ease? Is your vocal tone clear? Or does it sound thin and uncontrolled—breathy and without focus?

So the important thing is how you breathe—how you push air through your vocal folds. We will now have a look at the anatomy of breathing—again without getting too technical!

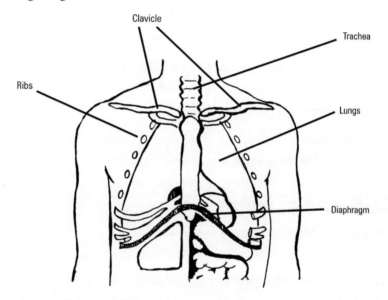

Figure 1.4
Chest, lungs, and diaphragm; when you breathe in, the diaphragm moves down and flattens out
PUBLISHED WITH PERMISSION OF JOSEPHINE ABBATANGELO

Anatomy of breathing
Lungs
The trunk of your body is separated into two compartments—your chest (where your ribcage, heart, and lungs are located), and your abdomen (containing your liver, intestines, and other organs).

In the chest, your ribcage is the protective casing around your lungs and heart. The muscles between the ribs are called the intercostal muscles. These contract and pull the ribs together—effectively raising them up and out when you breathe in. The intercostal muscles and the diaphragm (see below) open up your lungs to allow you to breathe in.

Diaphragm

Between your lungs and abdomen is a wide, flat muscle called the diaphragm. When it is at rest, the diaphragm is dome-shaped. When it contracts, it shortens from both sides. This causes it to flatten out and come down—effectively pulling the lungs down with it. The diaphragm is thus the main muscle of inhalation, and causes air to be sucked into the lungs.

When you breathe out, the diaphragm relaxes and returns to its original dome-shaped position. When this happens, the lungs are pushed back up, and air leaves the lungs through the windpipe.

For good singing technique, you need to develop all the muscles surrounding the breathing apparatus.

Coordinating the muscles

Have you noticed that when you sing your chest heaves upward, and your shoulders rise? Does your breath sound 'shallow'?

These are signs that you are not allowing your body to function efficiently. Or more accurately, the intercostal muscles and the diaphragm are not functioning efficiently.

Chapter 2
Posture and how to stand it

Chapter 2
Posture and how to stand it

Posture is basic to breathing

It is important to understand the benefits of good posture because it affects how you breathe—and, as we have seen, proper breathing is essential for singing. Few singers have properly understood how important good posture is for singing. If you sing flat, sharp, or with difficulty, you might think that it is always a problem with your voice. What has fascinated me most about correct singing technique is that many vocal problems are actually caused by poor posture—which leads to breathing difficulties and tenseness in the throat.

A simple test

Try singing a musical phrase with your neck protruding forwards and your head slightly elevated. Then sing the same line with your head in balance with the base of your spine, with your eyes looking directly ahead, and with your body feeling 'buoyant' (not rigid).

Which position is free of tenseness? The second position is much better of course—because your body is in alignment. Balance is essential.

Now you might think this is a little silly. But go to any pub on a Friday night and you'll notice that 'neck out and chin up' is how most people sing into a microphone. And they do this all night mind you—and probably a couple of other nights a week as well!

Think about your body as a huge generator of a power plant. If your generator is not working correctly—it obviously affects every department of the plant. It's the same with your body. Posture is important because, if you are standing in a way that hinders your breathing apparatus (especially your lungs and diaphragm), you will not be able to use them to their fullest potential.

Adopting the correct posture is important. Even a slight improvement in your posture can make a huge difference to your singing. I have had students come for one lesson on posture, followed by a week doing gigs, and they have been amazed at the length of time that they can now sing with comfort.

It pays to take a careful look at how your body is functioning—right now!

The Alexander technique
What is it?

The Alexander technique is a holistic method of finding out what your functional problems are, how they are affecting your breathing and your voice, and how you can correct these problem areas to improve your general health and wellbeing. It is a technique based on the importance of your neck, head, and spine being in correct alignment with the rest of your body.

How did it come about?

F. Matthias Alexander (1869–1955) was an Australian actor and reciter. He often suffered vocal strain and, at the end of his performances, he found that he could barely speak. He did not feel that he was doing anything wrong. In frustration, he set out to discover the cause of problems.

Alexander sought the advice of medical science, voice teachers, and other actors in his efforts to alleviate the problem—but all were unable to help him. The only thing that did work was not to speak at all. This, of course, was very frustrating and inconvenient!

Alexander set up a room with a number of mirrors at different angles so he could watch himself from every direction. At first he noticed nothing. However, after a while, he noticed that it wasn't while he was speaking that something was wrong—but before. In preparation for speaking, he found that he would tighten the back of his neck and pull his head back and down. In addition, he found that he was generally tense all over, which caused gasping breaths and constriction in his larynx.

How did it develop?

Alexander experimented for several years in attempts to change his habits. But, like all of us, he found the changes very difficult. The more he tried to change his ways, the more he noticed this same pattern of movements before he did anything! The way he stood, the way he sat down—it seemed that he carried a lot of tension which pulled his whole body out of alignment.

Despite the difficulties of making changes, over time Alexander did manage to eliminate all negative movement and unnecessary tension. The results were fascinating. His voice problems disappeared, and he also noticed that his health improved. Alexander was able to help many people—not just those with vocal difficulties, but also people with back, head, and neck problems. Alexander was able to help them all.

Conditions that can respond to the Alexander technique include:

• backache;

• vocal disorders and vocal cord nodules;

• stress;

• asthma;

• performance anxiety and anxiety attacks;

• functional disorders;

• temporo-mandibular joint (TMJ) disorder;

• migraine;

• tension headaches;

• rehabilitation after stroke, injury, operation, or other treatment;

• prevention of backache during pregnancy; and

• non-specific regional pain syndrome.

The results

Alexander achieved exceptional results, and ended up taking his work to London and America where he worked with many prominent performers, writers, and politicians. He wrote several books and, today, there are thousands of people who teach the Alexander technique all over the world.

How to make it work for you

A simple exercise

Here is a simple exercise for you to try out at home.

1. Stand with your back adjacent to a wall with your heels about five centimetres in front of the wall, and feet about half a metre apart. Do not lean against the wall.

2. Sway your body back towards the wall, but still keep your toes on the ground. Which part of your body hits the wall first—your shoulder blades or your backside?

3. Now aim to allow both your backside and your shoulder blades hit the wall at the same time. By now we can begin to identify what some of your problems are. There might be a gap between your lower back and the wall. This gap will disappear if you bend both your knees slightly forwards. Keep your heels on the ground.

4. While you are doing this, 'drop' your backside (if you can) and tilt your pelvis more towards the front rather than towards the floor. Make sure your head doesn't make contact with the wall.

5. Imagine that you have a piece of string attached to the top of your head and that someone is pulling this string from above, lifting you upwards. Feel your upper body rise as your chest opens up, but do not allow your feet to leave the floor.

6. Once you have done this, walk the length of the room retaining this posture.

What does all this mean?

By now you will have noticed where your problems lie.

• If your shoulder blades hit the wall first, it could be because your pelvis is carried too far forwards. You might find that you suffer middle-back pain.

• If your buttocks hit the wall first, it's probably the top part of your body which is slouched forwards.

I have noticed that very thin people tend to carry their pelvis too far forwards, and nearly always have middle back pain. This is through placing excessive pressure on the pelvis, thus throwing the spine and body balance out of alignment.

Tall people tend to hunch forwards (because everyone is shorter than they are!), and this results in shoulder or upper-back pains. I have also noticed that large-chested women and 'early developers' also have this problem (not to mention drummers!). These stereotypes are not true in every case, but the generalisations are a useful guide to common problems.

As you begin to change your habits you might feel a little uncomfortable at first. This is not because you are doing something wrong. It is because it takes time for your muscles to adapt.

Some examples of incorrect and correct posture

Here are some examples of incorrect and correct posture. By looking at these pictures and diagrams you should be able to pick up some valuable hints on what you are doing wrong—and how you can correct it.

Some examples when standing

Figures 2.1 and 2.2 (pages 28 and 29) show *incorrect* posture when standing. Figure 2.3 (pages 28 and 29) shows *correct* posture when standing.

Some examples when sitting

Figures 2.4 and 2.5 (page 30) show *incorrect* posture when sitting. Figure 2.6 (page 31) shows *correct* posture when sitting.

Some other things to remember

1. Always keep the balance of your body on the balls of your feet rather than on the heels. This relieves pressure on the base of your spine and also makes you stand with your pelvis well aligned.

2. Don't stand with your feet too far apart—in line with your shoulders is a good reference point.

3. I have found dancers tend to stand with their feet far apart, and placed in different positions—because this is how they are taught to stand for ballet. It's difficult to breathe when you stand like this because it upsets your body balance.

4. Some people stand with their feet so far apart that they can't breathe properly at all. Remember that all of the above comments on the Alexander technique refer to the ways in which your posture affects your breathing.

5. Make sure you are looking at something at eye level, so that your neck and chin don't lift upward.

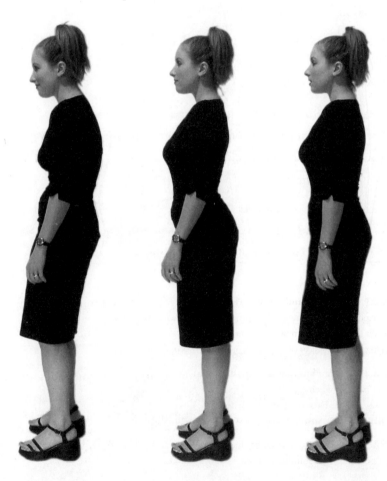

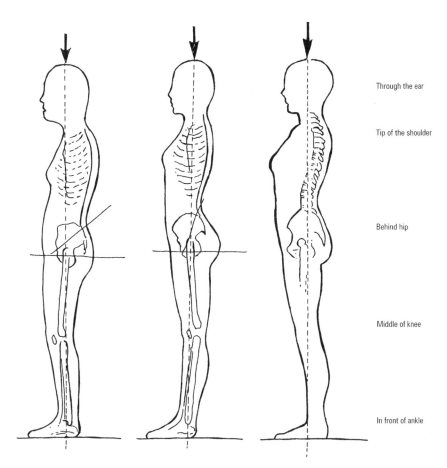

Through the ear

Tip of the shoulder

Behind hip

Middle of knee

In front of ankle

Figure 2.1 (Left photo and left diagram)
Incorrect posture when standing—slumped back tilts pelvis backwards;
this causes lower-back pain and leg pain
PUBLISHED WITH PERMISSION OF BRENDAN IMER AND JOSEPHINE ABBATANGELO

Figure 2.2 (Centre photo and centre diagram)
Incorrect posture when standing—arched back tilts pelvis forwards;
this causes middle-back pain and leg pain
PUBLISHED WITH PERMISSION OF BRENDAN IMER AND JOSEPHINE ABBATANGELO

Figure 2.3 (Right photo and right diagram)
Correct posture when standing—body is buoyant and balanced
PUBLISHED WITH PERMISSION OF BRENDAN IMER AND JOSEPHINE ABBATANGELO

Figure 2.4
Incorrect posture when sitting—shoulders hunched forwards and spine not in straight line; body lacks buoyancy
PUBLISHED WITH PERMISSION OF BRENDAN IMER

Figure 2.5
Incorrect posture when sitting—back arched and stiff and pelvis thrust forwards; spine distorted
PUBLISHED WITH PERMISSION OF BRENDAN IMER

Figure 2.6
Correct posture when sitting—body is buoyant and balanced
PUBLISHED WITH PERMISSION OF BRENDAN IMER

Some final thoughts on the Alexander technique

Although tenseness problems extended throughout his body, Alexander found that they always began in his neck and head. Because your neck, head, and torso have a controlling influence over the posture of rest of your body, it is important to be aware of tenseness in these areas.

I have been amazed at the results which the Alexander technique has brought to my colleagues and myself. There have been times in my classes when it seems that students are doing everything right as far as breathing is concerned, but they are still experiencing tenseness (and poor vocal resonance as a result). One minute 'against the wall' and their voices fly out with such ease that it shocks us all!

The message is—posture is *vitally* important!

Chapter 3

Breathing—the ins and outs

Chapter 3
Breathing—the ins and outs

Strength and coordination

When you sing or speak, there is ongoing interaction between your intercostal muscles (between the ribs, including your front, sides, and back), abdominal muscles (including the diaphragm), and laryngeal muscles (throat). They all naturally coordinate themselves without much thought from you. However, when these muscles are underdeveloped, and when their relationship with your head, neck and back is incorrect, you will experience difficulty in breathing for singing.

With regular exercise, you can strengthen these muscles and train them to coordinate, and you will find that they will respond more readily when needed. Like any sport that requires muscle strength—the more you work on a specific area, the greater the results.

In this chapter, we will take a look at some exercises that will strengthen these muscles. But before we start, let's take a look at some important information about breathing.

Three ways of breathing

There are basically three ways to breathe. These are:

- clavicular breathing;
- intercostal breathing; and
- abdominal breathing.

Clavicular breathing

Clavicular breathing results from lifting your shoulders. This does open the lungs, but it is a restricted way of expanding your lungs.

The clavicle is also called the 'collarbone'. It is situated just below your neck and runs parallel to the top of your breastbone (see Figure 3.1, page 36).

You should be able to feel it because it sticks out a little bit. Each collarbone is almost the same width as a shoulder.

Clavicular breathing results in a short, noisy breath, and people who breathe in this manner often complain of a feeling of insufficient breath.

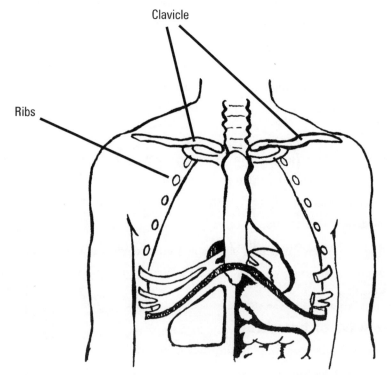

Figure 3.1
The clavicles (collarbones) are at the top of the chest
PUBLISHED WITH PERMISSION OF JOSEPHINE ABBATANGELO

Intercostal breathing

Intercostal breathing can be described as a breath taken basically by your chest. Your intercostal muscles (which are between your ribs) pull the ribs up and out, and thus help to expand the ribcage to allow space for lung expansion. See Figure 3.2, page 37.

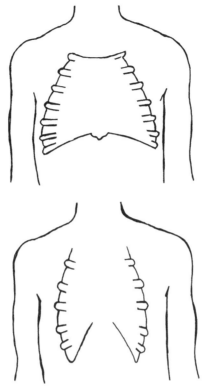

Figure 3.2
The intercostal muscles help to expand the ribcage and thus allow space for lung expansion
PUBLISHED WITH PERMISSION OF JOSEPHINE ABBATANGELO

Abdominal breathing

Abdominal breathing uses the diaphragm and allows you to take a really deep breath. The diaphragm contracts down (and flattens out) when you breathe in. This pushes against the abdominal organs, thus opening up the chest and allowing full expansion of your lungs. When you relax and breathe out, the diaphragm returns to its natural dome shape. Then there is a slight pause before the cycle begins again. See Figure 3.3, page 38.

You can also force air out of your lungs by pressing with your abdominal muscles (your 'abs'), thus pushing the abdominal organs upwards against the diaphragm and chest.

The diaphragm goes through its contraction and relaxation cycle naturally, but you can strengthen the surrounding abdominal muscles when you practise abdominal breathing and therefore improve your singing technique.

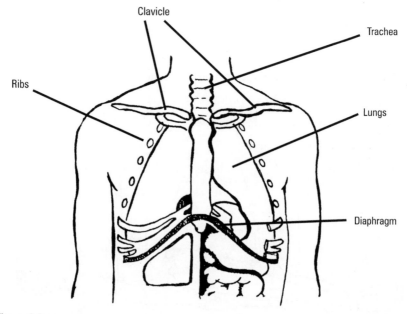

Figure 3.3
The diaphragm contracts down against the abdominal organs, allowing full expansion of the lungs when you breathe in
PUBLISHED WITH PERMISSION OF JOSEPHINE ABBATANGELO

So which way should you breathe?

Correct breathing for singing is a combination of intercostal breathing and abdominal breathing. Let's look at some exercises that improve these muscle groups. But first some general advice.

First things first

The best way to practise is to watch yourself in front of a full-length mirror. It's easier to see incorrect breathing patterns, and you can then readily correct yourself quickly.

Some breathing exercises
Exercise 1: Book on floor
This is a very simple exercise that will give you an understanding of how the trunk of your body should feel when using correct breathing. See Figures 3.4 and 3.5, below.

1. Lie completely flat on the floor.

2. Place a medium-sized book on your abdomen just underneath your rib cage. (The book should be about A5 paper size.)

3. Take in a deep breath so that the book rises. Make sure that the expansion is also felt in your ribcage.

4. Hold for three seconds, then release.

5. Repeat several times.

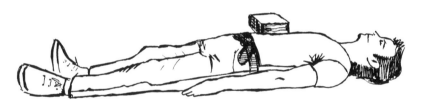

Figure 3.4
Exercise 1: Lie flat with a book on your abdomen …
PUBLISHED WITH PERMISSION OF JOSEPHINE ABBATANGELO

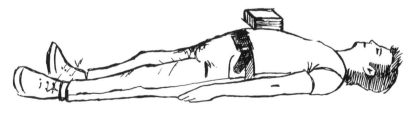

Figure 3.5
Exercise 1 (continued): Now take in a deep breath so that the book rises; make sure that there is simultaneous expansion of the ribcage
PUBLISHED WITH PERMISSION OF JOSEPHINE ABBATANGELO

Exercise 2: Ssh ...

Figure 3.6
Exercise 2: Stand straight with one hand on the side of your ribcage, and the other hand at the front over your diaphragm area

Exercise 2: Ssh …

This is one of the most effective exercises for strengthening the muscle groups you use for breathing.

1. Stand straight with one hand on the side of your ribcage, and the other hand at the front, just underneath your ribcage over the diaphragm area. (See Figure 3.6, page 40).

2. To understand the sensation of this breathing exercise, pretend that you are blowing out a candle placed in front of you. Feel the movements as you do this. Upon exhalation you will feel a muscular release around your abdominal and lower ribcage area. (Make sure that your sternum remains elevated as you do this, and that your neck remains straight and relaxed without jolting forward.)

3. Try this again, and watch what your body is doing. Is your chest collapsing? Is your neck jolting forward? Are your knees in a 'locked', tense position? You will really need to watch yourself to make sure that these things are not happening.

4. Now pretend to blow out a candle again, and say 'ssh … ' as you exhale. Remember that blowing out a candle is quick movement, and you should be feel your diaphragm and abdominal muscles work as you release the 'ssh'. Immediately after this, allow your muscles to return to their neutral position.

5. Take a full breath and release as above, this time using two 'ssh … ssh' sounds. Remember, each time it should be quick—like blowing out a candle.

6. Now repeat the pattern with three sounds of 'ssh … ssh … ssh'. Do this three times in succession.

7. Begin again, this time with a different consonant sound. Say 'vvv … ' Do this once, then twice, then three times.

8. Repeat the exercise again, this time with a different consonant sound. Say 'zzz … '.

9. Remember to make sure your chest is not caving in and that you are standing straight, but not rigid! Watch yourself like a hawk!

Exercise 3: Alphabet

1. Inhale as described in Exercise 2 (the 'ssh ... ' exercise).

2. Repeat the letters of the alphabet in your normal speaking voice, without allowing your ribcage to collapse; stay buoyant.

3. See how far you can go! If you get to Z start again.

Exercise 4: Counting

1. Inhale as described in Exercise 2 (the 'ssh ... ' exercise).

2. Count from 1 to 10 in your normal speaking voice, without allowing your ribs to relax. Inhale again and repeat.

3. Do this several times.

4. Finally, continue counting until your ribs and lungs are relaxed.

Exercise 5: Pregnant lady exercise

This is a very effective exercise and you will really feel your muscles working!

1. Take a short breath (but don't let your shoulders rise) as if you are about to blow out a candle (see the 'ssh ... ' exercise). Breathe out. Repeat this process as quickly as is comfortable.

2. It should feel as if you are panting like a puppy dog. (Those of you who have experienced labour, will understand this one straight away!)

3. If you release the breath quite quickly, you will feel the action of your breathing muscles really working in this exercise.

Some things to remember

Now you are on your way to developing your breathing. Well done! Let's just recap some important points that you must always keep in mind.

- Make sure you stand correctly (see Chapter 2 on posture). Your back should feel lengthened. Look straight ahead, and keep your neck relaxed, not rigid.

- Watch yourself in a full-length mirror.

- Remember that it is not *how much* you practise that is important—it's *how* you practise. It's better to get it right once than get it wrong ten times. Be patient with yourself and concentrate.
- Don't force anything.
- Enjoy yourself!

Chapter 4

Resonance and vibration

Chapter 4
Resonance and vibration

What are resonance and vibration?

By now you should be gaining a greater understanding of why good breath control is essential for correct vocal technique—and how to achieve it. This should be coupled with two other important factors—resonance and vibration. In this chapter I am going to talk about these important topics, and hope to shed some light on some terms you might have heard in relation to this area—but perhaps not fully understood.

The word *resonance* comes from a Latin word which means 'to resound'. When good resonance is present, your voice has a clear, bright ring to it. *Vibration* is the sensation created by resonance.

In modern music, there has been much confusion about what resonance is. This could be due to the fact that, with the invention of the microphone in the 1920s, singers began to rely less on their bodies for amplification. It is also actually more difficult to amplify a full, resonant voice electronically, so less resonant voices became more common. In addition, with the dawn of pop culture, singers were encouraged to use a lighter sound for radio—because it was easier to record. This led to the birth of 'crooning' in the style of Bing Crosby. However, these days, to meet the rigours of rock music, professional singers are again expected to have a loud, resonant voice.

So, for those of you who have never understood resonance, I will try to explain it as best I can.

Resonance and vibration are natural!

Resonance and vibration are parts of the natural course of singing and speaking—so you have probably already experienced them. Your job as a singer is to increase this natural resonance and the sensation of vibration which it brings. You do this first by understanding what resonance is, and then by experimenting through a series of exercises. In time, you will be able to apply these exercises to everything you sing.

Let's look at resonance and vibration separately so as to understand them better.

> **What are they?**
>
> **Resonance**
> Resonance enhances sound; it colours and amplifies your voice.
>
> **Vibration**
> Vibration is the sensation that sound produces in the bone structure of your face, head, and chest.

Resonance

The source of sound is your breath passing through your vocal folds, but it is the *vocal tract* that creates the colour and amplification of your voice that we call 'resonance'.

The vocal tract consists of:

- the oral and nasal pharynx;
- the nasal cavity; and
- the mouth.

See Figure 4.1, below, for a simplified diagram of the vocal tract.

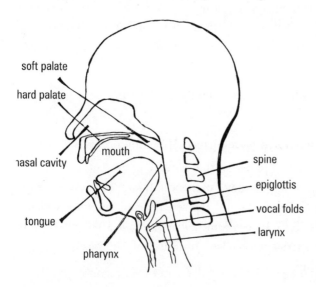

soft palate
hard palate
nasal cavity
mouth
tongue
pharynx
spine
epiglottis
vocal folds
larynx

Figure 4.1
Simplified diagram
of the vocal tract

PUBLISHED WITH PERMISSION
OF JOSEPHINE ABBATANGELO

These are what we call the 'resonating chambers'. Air vibrates through all these chambers simultaneously, not separately. This is what is called 'resonator coupling'. The shape and size of the vocal tract determines the *quality* of sound.

Oral and nasal pharynx

The oral pharynx is the space in the throat above your larynx and vocal folds. The nasal pharynx is the space above your soft palate, reaching up towards your nasal cavity.

Nasal cavity

The nasal cavity is the space behind your nose. The sinuses will be discussed when we talk about vibration later on in the chapter (see page 50).

Mouth

The interesting thing about your mouth (and soft palate as well for that matter) is that you can change their shape. To feel this, take a big yawn and you will feel your soft palate rise and stretch at the back of your throat.

You can also experience the change in shape of your mouth, tongue, and soft palate by slowly saying the five Italian vowels:

• A = 'AH'
• E = 'AY'
• I = 'EE'
• O = 'OH'
• U = 'OO'

Vibration

Vibration is the sensation created by resonance. Vibration occurs in:

• your sinuses; and

• your chest.

Vibration occurs when the frequency of the sound of your voice causes vibration in the bone structure of your face and chest.

See Figure 4.2, page 50, for a simplified diagram of your sinuses.

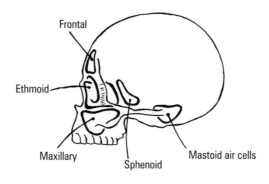

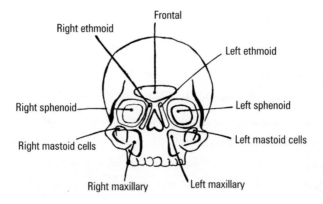

Figure 4.2
Simplified diagram of the sinuses
PUBLISHED WITH PERMISSION OF JOSEPHINE ABBATANGELO

Sinuses

The sinuses are spaces (like caves) in the bones of the skull, located in the cheekbones and above the eyes. They include the frontal sinuses, the sphenoid sinuses, and the anterior and posterior ethmoid cells, which are further back in the skull (see Figure 4.2).

You might notice when you have a head cold or hayfever that the quality of your voice changes—it loses a lot of its brightness and can sound dull. This is because the sinuses and/or nose are inflamed and blocked. We don't realise how much of our voice does reverberate in this area until we are sick with the 'flu or something similar!

In fact, it is sometimes said that if you had no head, your voice would sound like that of a duck! (Of course, we won't be trying any experiments to prove that theory—you'll just have to trust me!)

Chest

Some resonance does come from this area, but not as much as the above-mentioned sinus resonators. In fact, it is really only in classical singing that the chest is used to add colour to your voice. It is mainly the face and head area which produces resonance—hence the term 'head voice'. In rock and pop music, chest voice *is* used a lot, but volume, clarity, and strength of the voice can be achieved by using head voice.

Some questions

'If this is so natural, how come I need to learn it?'

Good question! Although resonance and vibration are parts of the natural course of singing and speaking, bad habits can mean that you are not using resonance and vibration to their fullest potential. If you become aware of this, you can learn how to implement and develop resonance and vibration to your advantage.

Opening your mouth too wide, clenching your jaw, not allowing your soft palate to rise—all these things can interfere with the true resonance and vibration of your voice. You might not even realise that you are doing these things because you have been doing them for so long.

'Why should I learn to sing this way?'

Another good question! When you concentrate on increasing resonance, it is possible to create clarity and volume in your voice without pressure. It is a pleasure to sing in this way because it's comfortable, and so much easier. We truly make it hard for ourselves by our well-established bad habits. Just ask my singing teacher!

It's all about becoming a *thinking* singer. If you can learn to concentrate so that you direct your voice to improve resonance and vibration, you will increase the sensation of what you are singing, and the ease of doing it. This is what *placement* means.

In the next chapter, you will find some exercises that will help get you started.

Chapter 5

Exercises for resonance and vibration

Chapter 5
Exercises for resonance and vibration

How to experience vibration for yourself

As we go through these exercises you will, at some point, experience resonance and vibration—because they are natural parts of singing. You will also enjoy doing this—because they make singing a lot easier!

The exercises

Exercise 1: 'Hmm ... '

1. Close your mouth and press your lips together. Allow your lower jaw to fall naturally (that is, do not clench your jaw).

2. Stand straight and breathe in, expanding your ribcage. Your diaphragm will move out and slightly down.

3. Sing the scale shown in Figure 5.1 (below). Sing 'Hmm ... '. Keep the vibration always in exactly the same place—your mouth and nose.

4. Go up the scale to a comfortable note, and then descend. Remember—keep the buzzing sensation!

5. Don't forget to breathe comfortably, and do not allow your shoulders to rise and fall. Let your torso accommodate your breathing, thinking about all-round expansion.

Figure 5.1
Exercise 1: Scale for 'Hmm ... '

Exercise 2: The witch

We have all heard the cackling laugh of the Wicked Witch of the West! If done properly, it is a great sound for really feeling the vibration of your voice.

1. Sit straight on the edge of a chair so that the base of your spine is supporting your upper body. Keep your hands by your side. See Figure 5.2, below.

Figure 5.2
Exercise 2: Sit straight on the edge of a chair so that the base of your spine is supporting your upper body
PUBLISHED WITH PERMISSION OF JOSEPHINE ABBATANGELO

2. Bend forwards so that your head is between your legs, and so that your arms are hanging by each side of your legs. Try not to be tense, and try to breathe as naturally as you can. See Figure 5.3.

Figure 5.3
Exercise 2: Bend forwards so that your head is between your legs, and so that your arms are hanging by each side of your legs
PUBLISHED WITH PERMISSION OF JOSEPHINE ABBATANGELO

3. OK, here comes the silly bit! Pronounce the sound 'Heh! Heh! Heh!'. Direct this to the area where you feel a pulsation in your upper face and forehead. If you are doing this correctly, you will feel a vibration in the area of your face area. The sound will be quite loud, without any force or pressure.

4. If you are feeling it in the throat, try focusing more on the initial 'H' sound of the 'Heh!', and allow your breathing to feel free as you do this.

5. Once you feel you have it right, sit up straight away, and make the sound again. Make sure you are not tensing your face. Keep as relaxed as you can.

Exercise 3: 'Hmm … vee … '

1. Start on a note that's comfortable—not too high, and not too low.

2. Start with 'hmm … ', feeling the vibration at your lips and/or the mask of your face.

3. On the same breath, change from 'Hmm … ' to 'Vee … ' keeping the feeling of the vibration of the sound in the same place.

4. Sustain the note for about two or three seconds.

5. Continue up the scale by semitones, keeping the feeling of the vibration in the same place. Your voice should have a bright ring to it, and you should not experience any tension. (Do *not* clench your jaw or face— stay relaxed.)

6. Once you have gone up the scale to a high note (it should be comfortably high and not difficult), descend the scale by semitones to a comfortable low note.

Exercise 4 The glide

This exercise is also good for strengthening pitch and register breaks.

1. On the vowel 'Ooo … ' glide up and down the scale, starting in the upper part of your register—but not too high (just wherever is comfortable).

2. Make sure that you feel the 'buzz' in your face. If you don't feel a 'buzz', try 'Mmmooo … '. First feel the 'buzz' on your lips as you begin with the 'Mmm … ', and then concentrate on keeping the sensation there for the vowel (' … ooo').

3. Once you feel you have it, try it again with 'Ooo … '. Then slowly glide down the scale on 'Uuu … ' to a comfortable low note, then ascend to a comfortable high note.

4. Your aim throughout this whole exercise is to feel the *vibration* of sound in the same place. Because you will be gliding up and down, it is easy for the colour of your voice to change. For example, in the lower notes, it might become 'breathy' or husky. Try to allow your voice to sound consistent and even. Imagine you are singing in a straight line ahead of you—not going up and down. Keep the tone smooth, and feel the 'buzz'!

Chapter 6

Vocal warm-ups

Chapter 6
Vocal warm-ups

Like an athlete

Athletes warm up their bodies before they compete. In a similar way, your voice should be sufficiently warmed up for the 'sport' of singing. In this chapter you will find some simple scales that should take 15–30 minutes to do.

As with all exercises, it is important that these vocal warm-ups be done correctly. Otherwise they will be of little help to you. Here are some tips to make sure you stay 'on track'.

Some common questions

What note should I start these scales on?

I have started all these scales on middle C, but you can start wherever your voice feels comfortable. This will be different for different voices. Make sure you start on a note that is comfortable (but not too low), and then go as high and as low as possible without straining your voice.

I have given each scale only in a starting key. Continue the progression until you reach your top note, and then descend the scale to a comfortable low note.

How long should I take to warm up?

Between 15 and 30 minutes should be sufficient. It should take no longer than half an hour. Take little breaks of a few minutes in between certain exercises. Have a glass of water in these breaks, do some stretches, and relax.

When should I warm up?

If you can get into the discipline of warming-up in the morning, you will find that your voice will be better throughout the course of the day. This is because you are starting the day with correct placement of the voice—which should enable you to speak and sing correctly from start to finish.

It is a dangerous practice to speak low and 'breathy' all day if you are tired, and then expect that a warm-up just before your performance will fix everything. It won't—it will just make your voice even more tired. So have some breakfast, have a shower (or whatever it takes to wake you up!)—and then go for it!

If I warm up in the morning, should I warm up before a gig as well?

Yes, you should. If your gig is later in the day or in the evening, warm up in the morning. Then, an hour before your performance, do some light warm-ups. This should take about 10–15 minutes if you have disciplined yourself to warm-ups in the mornings.

How do I know if I'm practising correctly?

In every exercise, you should feel the vibration of your voice in the mask of your face. You might feel it strongly in your nose and cheekbones—as long as you feel some sensation in this area you will know that you are singing correctly. (For more information on this, see Chapters 4 and 5 on resonance and vibration.)

Your voice should sound resonant, and you should feel a slight 'buzzing' in your head. This might take a lot of concentration at first, but it will become easier as you practise regularly.

How can I get the most benefit from my warm-ups?

Here are some hints on how to get the most out of your warm-ups:

* practise in front of a mirror;

* record your scales on tape;

* use placement imagery to help you relax; and

* have a glass of water handy.

Let's talk about each of these ideas.

Practise in front of a mirror

The best way to practise is standing in front of a full-length mirror. This way you can keep an eye on your posture and your breathing. Don't warm up in the car unless you absolutely have to. Because you are sitting down, you will not be able to breathe correctly—and you will not be able to give full concentration to your singing technique. This is a lazy warm up!

If you put one hand on the side of your ribcage and one hand over your diaphragm area, you will feel what your body is doing when you are breathing. You will know whether you are doing things correctly. (See Figure 6.1, below.)

Remember that your breathing is the 'fuel' for your voice.

Figure 6.1
The best way to practise is in front of a full-length mirror

Record your scales on tape

If you don't have a piano or cannot read music, get your teacher or a friend to put suggested scales in your range onto tape. This is the best way to practise. Not only does it leave you free to concentrate on your technique, but also (especially if you are touring), you can take it with you and keep to a routine.

Use placement imagery to help you relax

Try to think 'horizontally' instead of 'vertically' when you are practising. (For more information on the meaning of these terms, see Chapter 7 on placement imagery.)

Have a glass of water handy

Have a glass of water handy so that you can have a sip between exercises. This will keep your throat hydrated. You can use other drinks, but do not drink anything too hot or too cold. I often have a herbal tea—just make sure that it's not too hot!

How often should I warm up?

If you are singing all the time, a warm-up five or six times a week will be very beneficial. I often have a day off to give my voice a rest. Or if I don't have a lot of gigs, I don't warm up for a couple of days—so that I can have a break (although this is very rare!).

If you want to see an improvement in the quality and longevity of your voice, I suggest a daily routine. I actually enjoy warming up—because my voice feels so good afterwards. I feel like I'm spoiling myself!

Can I use these scales indefinitely instead of getting my own teacher?

No, this is not a good idea. Although these scales are very simple, and you might think that you don't need a teacher to tell you these things, it really is important to have your own teacher who can guide you personally, and correct you when you go wrong. The warm-up ideas that I have given you here are just designed to be examples that will help you get into a routine. You really need a teacher to give you personalised guidance.

I still use a majority of these exercises, but I vary my warm-up scales depending on what needs to be developed in my voice. (Yes, even professional singers need to continually work on improving!)

Also keep in mind that this is a light warm-up—something you can do every day if you are gigging a lot. However, your schedule will change throughout the year—and so should your warm-up. A teacher is the best person to guide you through your changing requirements.

Some vocal warm-ups

Warm-up 1: 'Bww ... '

You know the sound you make when you are freezing— 'Bww ... it's cold!'. This is the sound you want to make in this warm-up. You should feel a buzzing and vibration on your lips. Figure 6.2 shows the scale for this.

Figure 6.2
Warm-up 1: Scale for 'Bww ... '

Warm-up 2: 'Brr ... '

Perhaps when you are cold, you say 'Brr ... ' (rather than 'Bww ... '). Repeat the above warm-up exercise, this time using 'Brr ... '. Make sure you roll the 'rr's. Again, feel the vibration in the front of the face. Figure 6.3 shows the scale for this.

Figure 6.3
Warm-up 2: Scale for 'Brr ... '

Warm-up 3: 'Hmm ... '

Close your mouth and press your lips together. Make the sound 'Hmm ... ', directing the vibration of sound to the front of your face. You should feel a slight buzzing on your lips, in your mouth, and in your nose. Sing the scale, concentrating on keeping the feeling of the sound in the same place. Go as high as is comfortable and as low as is comfortable. Figure 6.4 shows the scale for this.

Hmmm

Figure 6.4
Warm-up 3: Scale for 'Hmm ... '

Warm-up 4: Some others to go on with

Now continue warming-up with the following exercises, keeping in mind that you should always feel the vibration in the front of your face.

Because you will now have the idea, I won't give detailed instructions for each one of the following exercises. I'll just number them as 4a, 4b, 4c, and so on. You can work through them yourself. As I mentioned previously, I have given each scale only in a starting key. Continue the progression until you reach your top note, and then descend the scale to a comfortable low note.

Good luck!

Warm-up 4a: 'Vee ... '

Vee _____ Breath   Vee _____

Figure 6.4a
Warm-up 4a: Scale for 'Vee ... '

Warm-up 4b: 'Vi … vee … vah … '

Vi Vi Vi Vi Vi Vi Vi Vee _____ Vah _____ *Breath*

Figure 6.4b
Warm-up 4b: Scale for 'Vi … vee … vah … '

Warm-up 4c: 'Vee … ah … ' (No. 1)

Vee _____ Ah _____

Figure 6.4c
Warm-up 4c: Scale for 'Vee …ah …' (No. 1)

Warm-up 4d: 'Vee … ah … ' (No. 2)

Vee _____ Ah _____

Figure 6.4d
Warm-up 4d: Scale for 'Vee … ah … ' (No. 2)

Warm-up 4e: 'Ska … '

Figure 6.4e
Warm-up 4e: Scale for 'Ska … '

Warm-up 4f: 'Vee … ay … ah … '

Figure 6.4f
Warm-up 4f: Scale for 'Vee … ay … ah … '

Chapter 7
Placement imagery

Chapter 7
Placement imagery

The act of thinking

There is a way of thinking that can help you to break formed habits that prevent you singing well. Changing thought patterns can significantly change the way you sing. I often think 'in pictures' to help me break bad habits that prevent me singing with ease. This way of thinking is what is called 'placement imagery'.

This idea is not new to singing, although few people utilise it. I want to share some of my 'pictures' with you in the hope that they will help you reduce any tension that you might have in the throat and body.

It is often easy to see in a singer's face what he or she is thinking when approaching a difficult section of a song. For example, when reaching for high notes, does the neck come forward, is the jaw tense, and do the eyebrows lift? I have even seen some people stand on their toes! I have done all of these things myself. These habits are often not noticed by the singer, or by anyone else—unless someone is watching for them! Nevertheless, these are the very things that prevent agility and ease when singing.

> **Two important hints**
> When it comes to inventing 'pictures' to help you with your thinking, keep two things in mind.
>
> • It is really important that you have a good singing teacher who can guide you in the right direction. Everyone needs outside guidance for best results.
>
> • You will also find that different pictures work for different people—so put your creative 'thinking cap' on. You will surprise yourself.

Some imagery exercises

In this part of the chapter, we will talk about some useful images for:

- breathing;
- high notes;
- low notes; and
- placement.

Breathing

Ice-cream cone

Pretend that you have a large 'upside-down' ice-cream cone inside the trunk of your body—from your breastbone down to your abdomen and pelvis. See Figure 7.1, below.

When you breathe in, imagine that the cone is filling up from the point of the cone (at the breastbone) right down to the bottom (in your abdomen and pelvis). Do this slowly—to be aware of expansion in your lungs all the way down to your diaphragm and abdominal area.

Figure 7.1
Pretend that you have a large 'upside-down' ice-cream cone inside the trunk of your body
PUBLISHED WITH PERMISSION OF JOSEPHINE ABBATANGELO

Hollow legs

Imagine that your legs are made of hollow pieces of wood. When you breathe in, imagine that you are filling up your legs with air—right down to the very tips of your toes.

High notes

The bottomless pit

Imagine that you are standing on the edge of a bottomless pit. Every high note you sing is falling down into the pit—so far below that you can't even see where the note has gone.

The little ant

If you are singing a song which is generally high this is a good thought to conjure up. Imagine you are a tall giant and that there is a tiny little ant on the floor in front of you (see Figure 7.2). Sing to the little ant!

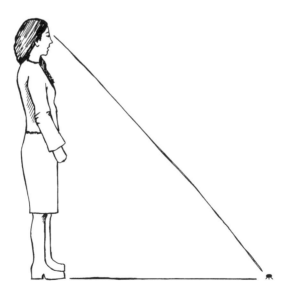

Figure 7.2
Imagine you are a tall giant and that there is a tiny little ant on the floor in front of you
PUBLISHED WITH PERMISSION OF JOSEPHINE ABBATANGELO

The flip-top lid and the bird

If I have to sing a note that is right at the top end of my range, this one is great. Imagine that the top part of your head has a flip-top lid! Imagine that this lid is hinged at the back and opens from your forehead upward. Whenever a note is very high, imagine that the lid pops open and that your note is a bird that flies away. Just let it fly away—don't push it out. Let the note come out freely and fly away.

Low notes

The clouds

You are sitting on a fluffy white cloud high above the earth. You can see heaven high above you in the sky—and all the angels are trying to hear your sing! Allow your notes to reach right up into to the highest heavens.

The ladder

For every low note you sing going down your range, pretend that you are climbing one rung up a ladder. If the note is really low, imagine that the ladder is going right through the roof, and that you are at the very top.

Placement

Here are some images to help you with placement of your voice. The first one ('the clothesline') is the thought I most commonly use.

The clothesline

Imagine you have a clothesline attached to the middle of your ear. It extends far behind you—perhaps several metres if you are singing very high. See Figure 7.3, page 75.

Every note you sing is a peg on the clothesline. The low notes represent the pegs closest to your ear. As you sing higher, each peg is moving further away from you on the clothesline—which means that the highest note you sing is as far behind you as possible.

This image helps not to push to increase volume. It assists in keeping your tone even and in the 'same place'.

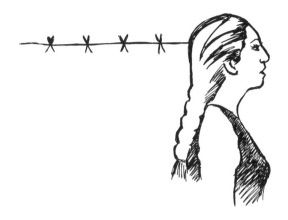

Figure 7.3
Imagine you have a clothesline extending far behind you

Pinocchio

Imagine that you have a very long pointy nose like Pinocchio (Figure 7.4). Whether you are singing high or low, mentally anticipate that every note you sing sits right on the tip of your nose. Place every note in exactly this same place.

Figure 7.4
Imagine that you have a very long pointy nose like Pinocchio

Bull's eye

Pretend you have a dartboard about ten centimetres in front of your face. Imagine that every note you sing hits the bull's eye.

Some final thoughts on imagery

These are just a few pictures that I use. In doing this sort of thought practice, you might feel a little strange at first. But you will be surprised at the difference it makes. In time, you will come up with your own pictures—different thoughts work for different people.

Always watch yourself in a mirror to see what your body is doing during a difficult section of a song or scale. You might observe that you are doing some strange things! See what happens when you change your thought patterns. For example, if you stick your neck out when singing, try thinking in pictures. Observe carefully in the mirror. Is there a change in sound and appearance? A combination of watching yourself and thinking in pictures should prevent problems from occurring.

Have fun!

Chapter 8

Vocal registers
and voice classification

Chapter 8
Vocal registers and voice classification

What is a vocal register?
A complicated topic
The topic of vocal registers and voice classification is a complicated one, and there are many varying opinions on the subject. I suggest that you try to understand as much as you reasonably can—and then not concern yourself too much if there are a few grey areas. As you study singing and better understand your own voice, you will find that certain aspects of this chapter will become clearer over time.

Making smooth transitions
A vocal register can be described as a group of notes in your range that have the same sound quality and which 'feel' the same when you sing. Your voice has three main registers—*chest register, middle register, and head register* (or *head voice*).

You might notice when you approach certain notes in your range that the 'colour' of your voice changes or feels different. There might also be an obvious pitch break—at which the quality and sensation of your voice changes noticeably. This is your voice-changing registers. *Passaggio* is the word used to describe this area of change.

As a disciplined singer, it is your job to make these transitions as smooth as possible, so that the listener cannot hear obvious breaks or extreme changes in timbre (quality of the voice). In other words, the vocal line of sound should be even and matched in quality. These register changes will always be there—that is, you will always feel the change. But you can train your voice to keep the transition indiscernible to your listener's ear.

Voice classification
What is voice classification?
Voice classification is your complete vocal range—and what category matches your range. These categories include soprano, alto, and so on. A combination of timbre (sound quality) and your own comfortable vocal range generally determines the classification of your voice.

People sometimes find classification difficult. Because every voice is different, the individual sound and range needs to be evaluated by expert ears. Keep in mind that voice classification is something that is used as a guide to group voices in the best possible way. And remember that sometimes amazing voices break all the rules!

I am going to simplify voice classification as much as possible. Normally pop and rock arrangements group voices into three parts. Often the soprano parts are not as high as you find in classical composition.

The main classifications

The main voice classifications are shown in Table 8.1.

Female	Male
soprano	tenor
mezzo soprano	baritone
alto	bass

Table 8.1
The main voice classifications

Again, I must stress that this is simplified. Within each register, there are also other classifications to describe timbre (sound quality) and colour of the voice. For example, within the soprano register, there are dramatic sopranos, lyrical sopranos, coloratura sopranos, and so on. These terms are not really used in the pop and rock music genres.

Figure 8.1 (page 81) shows a simple chart with basic register ranges.

FM grouping

You will notice from Figure 8.1 that soprano/tenor, mezzo soprano/baritone, and alto/bass, are similar in their range of notes—except that the male ranges are an octave lower than their female counterparts. This is good to keep in mind when you are working out group parts, as you will find it easier to group male and female voices together (give or take a few notes). It is useful to think in this way because three groups are much easier to organise than six! I call this 'FM grouping' (female–male grouping).

Although simple three-part harmony structures tend to be the most common arrangements, this is not always the case with every song arrangement. The basis for traditional choral and gospel work is generally four vocal parts. These are soprano, alto, tenor, and bass.

In some arrangements, there can be as many as five or six parts. In these cases, you will find that often there are basic three-part harmonies, but that certain notes change between FM groupings. For example, an alto part might move up and down a scale quite a lot, but its FM group—which is bass— might not move as much (although they might mainly sing a similar part). There will be a few slight changes—an octave lower, of course, because bass is a male voice. If you read music, you will notice these subtle changes—which make vocal arrangements intricate and interesting.

Figure 8.1
Chart of basic register ranges

Why is it important to understand vocal registers and voice classification?

Firstly, it will help you to classify your own voice. This is important for group singing. For example, if you are doing a studio session, a certain grouping of voices might be required. If everyone in the group is alto and bass there is not going to be much colour in the sound—because the timbre will be quite similar. It can also be difficult to find someone to sing various parts (such as higher parts). The parts need to be balanced.

Secondly, if you are the one who is organising a group of singers, a knowledge of registers will help you to know who to group together, and where to place them. This saves time and energy, and also gives you a greater understanding of the parts that will work well. You will also have a greater understanding of how high or low each group can go according to its register classification.

And, finally, you will also be able to discern which type of voice is needed for a certain piece of music—especially when a solo voice is required for a project.

Can there be an 'overlapping' of notes in voice classification?

Yes. Classifications are only a guide, and every voice is different. You might find that your voice does not extend the complete range of a register, or that it overlaps into another register. It is quite common for sopranos to sing mezzo soprano or alto parts—although their main strength lies in their soprano register. The same applies to all registers.

Chest, middle, and head voice
What do these terms mean?

Now that you have an understanding of vocal registers and voice classification, let's talk about chest voice, middle voice, and head voice You might have heard these terms used before, but might not have quite understood them fully.

There is a lot of confusion about this topic. Most people think of 'head voice' as being a very high operatic soprano-type voice, or might use the term to describe someone singing very light and high—but this is not what it really means. People sometimes say, 'I have a cold today, so I can sing only in head voice', or 'I can't 'belt' my higher notes out today, so I will do them in head voice'. This sort of talk infers that not much energy is required to sing in this way, or that head voice creates a light, thin sound—as opposed to a strong, thick voice.

So what do these terms really mean?

The real meaning of these terms relates to where the sensation and vibration of your voice is felt. For example, 'head voice' is a term used to describe the sensation of your voice being felt in your face and head area. Similarly, to sing in 'chest voice' means to feel the vibration of the voice in your chest area. (You will find more information about this subject in Chapters 4 and 5 on resonance and vibration.)

If you sing in both 'chest voice' (which includes what is called 'open' chest and 'chest mixture') and 'middle voice', this is called a *vocal mixture*—in which the vibration of your voice is felt in your chest, and the sensation of your voice is felt in the mask of your face.

So what is the right or best way to sing?

Again I must stress that you should always feel the sensation (resonance) of your voice in your head and face area. However, the vibration of your voice will change—depending on where you are singing in your register.

For example, a bass singer will predominantly feel the vibration of his voice in his chest because the notes are very low, but will still experience resonance in his head and face. A soprano will usually feel vibration in her head and face area for almost her whole range.

What do people mean by a 'vocal mixture'?

This is a term used to describe a quality of sound (timbre) which is not completely 'middle' and not completely 'chest'—but a mixture of both.

Remember that you always feel the resonance of your voice in the mask of your face, but the vibration of your voice can be felt in your chest in your lower register.

Can I use head voice throughout my whole register?

Yes, you can use 'head voice' throughout your whole register. Let me also say that to sing in this way creates a full, resonant vocal tone, with a lot of strength and clarity. However, as you sing your lower notes, you might feel the vibration of the voice in your chest.

As long as you are always experiencing the sensation of your voice in the mask of your face, you will know you are singing correctly—no matter how high or low your notes are.

Can I sing in chest voice throughout my whole register?

No, you cannot sing in 'chest voice' throughout your whole register. You can sing in 'chest voice' for part of your lower register, but it is not recommended to extend the chest register beyond the area of the *Passaggio.*

PART II
PERFORMANCE

Chapter 9

Live work

PUBLISHED WITH PERMISSION OF REBECCA DAVIES

Chapter 9
Live work

Commonsense, but easily neglected

In this chapter we are going to talk about microphones and monitors, solo and group singing, and good live work etiquette.

Some of this stuff is really just commonsense, but even the most advanced singer can sometimes neglect the basics. So let's start with microphones and monitors—with special emphasis on solo singing. Then we will say a few things about group singing and proper etiquette in live work.

Microphones in solo work

If you have an understanding of how your microphone works, you will have a greater appreciation of how to use it. So let's have a closer look at the singer's most common piece of equipment—the microphone—without getting too technical.

Diaphragms and polar patterns

There are two important terms which we need to describe:

- the diaphragm of a microphone; and
- the polar pattern of a microphone.

Diaphragms

All microphones have a diaphragm that determines how sound is converted or amplified. A diaphragm is a thin sheet of material inside a microphone. When sound waves reach the diaphragm, it vibrates to convert sound into electrical audio signals.

The shape of the diaphragm varies in different types of microphones, depending on what needs to be amplified. For example, a Shure SM58 microphone is most commonly used for live vocal work, whereas an SM57 is more suited to amplify certain instruments (for example, a guitar amp) The shape and size of the diaphragm varies accordingly.

Polar patterns

The term 'polar pattern' is used to explain the area of sound picked up a diaphragm. Different types of microphones have different pick-up patterns, and microphones are usually classified into groups, according to their particular polar patterns.

Types of microphone

Now that we have an idea of these terms ('diaphragm' and 'polar pattern') we can understand how microphones are classified.

Depending on their polar pattern, microphones can be classified into three types:

- uni-directional microphones;
- directional microphones; and
- omni-directional microphones.

Uni-directional microphones

The term 'uni-directional' refers to microphones with a narrow pick-up area. This group of microphones includes the types used most commonly for live performances—cardioid and hypercardioid microphones. We will discuss these cardioid and hypercardioid microphones in more detail below, but for now we can say that they fit into the category of uni-directional microphones in their polar patterns.

Directional microphones

The term 'directional' refers to microphones with a wider pick-up field than a narrow uni-directional microphone, but not as wide as the third type—an 'omni-directional' microphone (see below). Directional microphones basically pick up whatever you are directing them at. An example is the sort of microphones used in most video cameras.

Omni-directional microphones

The term 'omni-directional' refers to microphones which pick up all areas of sound. This type of microphone is commonly used in dramas and plays, or to record crowd noises. For example 'shotgun microphones' are used for choirs, and can be placed quite a distance away.

Cardioid and hypercardioid microphones

Now let's have a look at cardioid and hypercardioid microphones more closely to help you understand how they should be used, and why. As mentioned above, cardioid and hypercardioid microphones are the types used most commonly for live performances, and both are called 'uni-directional'—because they pick up sound from a narrow area.

Cardioid microphones

With cardioid microphones, the pick-up pattern (determined by the diaphragm) is shaped something like a 'heart'—that is, sound is picked up mainly from the front of the microphone, a little from the sides, and virtually nothing from behind. An example of a cardioid microphone is the trusted SM58, which is the most common microphone used for live gigs. This type of microphone is excellent for live solo work. Other cardiod microphones include radio microphones such as the AKG.

Hypercardioid microphones

Hypercardiod microphones still pick up most of the sound from the front, but the circumference of sound pick-up is much narrower. This is because the diaphragm is shaped like a heart squashed from the sides. It is therefore more narrow. Like a cardioid microphone, a hypercardiod microphone picks up a little from the sides, but virtually nothing from behind. These microphones are good for choirs, or a group of several singers, rather than for solo singing.

How to use a microphone

The angle of incidence

If you are not experienced in microphone technique it is best to keep it on the stand—especially if it has a lead. This keeps the space between the microphone and your mouth more consistent.

However, whether you keep it in the stand or hold it, it's not a good idea to have the microphone directly in front of your mouth at a 90-degree angle. This is because it increases popping sounds, excessive sibilance, and the sound of your breath. The ideal is to angle it at 10–15 degrees. This angle is called the 'angle of incidence'. It is better to sing over the head of the microphone, or to one side of it. See Figure 9.1, below.

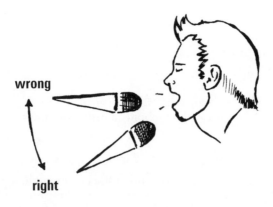

Figure 9.1
The angle of incidence—it is better to sing over the head of the microphone, or to one side of it
PUBLISHED WITH PERMISSION OF JOSEPHINE ABBATANGELO

The way it looks
For purely aesthetic reasons I do not like to see people singing with the microphone right in front of their mouths. It hides the expressions of the mouth and the lower face. This is more noticeable on television in which there are many close-up shots.

Sometimes I find it hard to understand what people are singing when I can't see their mouths. A significant part of a good performance lies with facial expression and being a good communicator. It is a shame when people let a piece of ugly equipment get in the way!

Distance

If you have been singing for a long time, you will already have your own idiosyncrasies when it comes to microphone technique. Some people like to have their lips sitting right on the top of the microphone, whereas others sing several centimetres away. When you start using a microphone all the time, you will probably notice that you do a bit of both—depending on what the song lends itself to.

You need to be aware of what is happening to the sound of your voice when you do these things. For example, 'eating' the microphone means that the audience hears absolutely everything. Any noise that you make is heard—good or bad! On the other hand, if you're too far away, this will make your voice sound 'thin'. The sound engineer will be constantly trying to amplify your voice above the band, and the possibility of feedback from the monitors increases because the engineer will have to turn your microphone up louder so you can be heard.

If you have your mouth a few centimetres away from the microphone, the engineer has full control, people can see your face, and you can concentrate only on the job of doing a good gig.

And whatever you do, make sure that you have consistency in your technique. It makes it easier for the front-of-house and foldback engineers, for your band, for yourself—and for your audience!

Monitors

Monitors—both on-stage monitors (foldback wedges) and in-ear monitoring—make life a whole lot easier for singers and musicians—so it is important to know how to use them to your advantage.

The importance of monitors in solo singing

It is very important to make sure you use monitors to their full advantage. You might have had the experience of doing a gig in which you had difficulty hearing yourself in the monitors. The response to this experience is usually to sing louder. This results in a tired voice, and also produces a terrible sound out the front! Proper use of monitors can get around this problem.

What should I have in my monitors?

Smaller venues

What you need in your monitor really depends on the size of the venue. For example, if you are singing in a smaller type of venue, you will be able to hear a lot of on-sound stage sound from the other instruments. This means you probably won't need the guitar and bass in your own wedge—because you will hear them directly from their amps (especially the guitarist!).

A good rule to follow in most situations is to have as little instrumentation as possible in your wedge. This is so you can hear yourself more clearly. For example, when I perform, I normally have my vocal, keyboards, backing tracks (for loops or extra parts), and a little bit of guitar in my wedge. If the songs are more guitar-orientated and if a lot of the song intros start with guitar, I make sure that I have more guitar. The most important thing is that I can hear my voice clearly.

Larger venues

If you are performing at a larger venue (one that seats several thousand people) your monitor set-up should be very different. In this situation, your band is likely to be more spread out over a larger stage. These types of venues are usually really 'boomy', and it is often difficult to hear true sound without hearing the echo of the auditorium. If your monitors are not set up properly, you will have difficulty in pitching. You might also have difficulty with keeping in time—because you might not hear what the drums are doing. It can be a very uncomfortable place to be!

In this situation, I have a lot more in my wedge. Vocal, tracks, keyboards, guitar, and the 'kick and snare' of the drums are all important. You could also consider the 'hi-hats' if a song starts with them. I never have the backing vocals or the extra percussion—because they are not needed.

The same rule still applies—have only what you need, and make sure you can hear yourself!

But what if I still can't hear myself?

If you still can't hear yourself, don't be afraid to 'hand signal' to the monitor guy that you need more of something. Actually, before doing this, make sure that you have met the monitor guy before you start the gig! These guys work really hard and often get treated pretty badly by bands. Good relationships with your front-of-house and monitor engineers are extremely important, and certainly helps with communicating what you want when you are in the middle of a performance.

If, after all this, you are still having trouble hearing yourself, never yell to increase your volume. Keep in mind that what you are hearing in your monitors is *not* what the audience is hearing. You might be able to hear yourself better when you 'push' to be heard—but all that they will hear is somebody screaming! It sounds ugly and it's hard work.

If I can't hear myself, and if I have done everything that I can to rectify the problem, I still sing at a volume that is comfortable. It is frustrating, but if you have done all you can and you are in the middle of a set, you have only two alternatives—either sing at a comfortable level, or scream! Much better to settle for a comfortable level!

Also, if I am having trouble pitching because of difficulty in hearing instrumentation, I walk over to the amp of an instrument (for example, a guitar) to hear what is happening.

Monitor EQ

You can usually change the EQ of your monitor mix. For example, I have a lot of high frequencies in my voice, so I like a lot more middle and bottom EQ so it doesn't cut my ears like razorblades! If you have a very husky thick voice, you might want higher frequencies to make your voice sound a bit more 'toppy' (higher frequencies) and less 'bottom end' (lower frequencies). The more you perform, the more you will learn what you like to hear and what you don't.

Monitor feedback

Your monitors will feed back if you direct the microphone towards them, or stand too close. Never face the microphone towards your monitors. If you do, your ears will take a beating (not to mention everybody else's!). When you have finished singing, if you have to put your microphone on the floor, rather that in its stand, face it towards you and away from the wedges.

In-ear monitoring

What are in-ear monitors?

If you have never used in-ear monitors before, the easiest way to explain them is to imagine that you are hearing things through 'Walkman-style' earphones. Basically, it's having your monitors as earplugs!

In-ear monitoring consists of two earplugs and a small transmitting unit. This transmitting unit clips onto your belt or another piece of suitable clothing. There is also a receiving unit at the mixing desk. Your unit has level controls, which you can adjust to suit your ears.

The advantages

In-ear monitors are definitely one of the best ways to hear yourself more clearly. This is because sound is entering your ears directly—like when you listen to a CD. It also means that you cut out a fair bit of unnecessary noise, and that you have personal control over sound and vocal levels. Most singers comment that they don't have to work so hard vocally because they can hear themselves more accurately. In-ear monitors also significantly reduce feedback, and have built-in limiters that prevent noise levels from peaking and blowing your ears off!

Another 'plus' is that you can move freely around the stage and have the same mix no matter where you are.

If you are travelling extensively, you can buy your own unit and take it with you. They are quite expensive—but they are worth the expense. If you think about it, most musicians spend thousands on their instruments and travel with their own gear. For a singer, having your own in-ear monitors is worth the money.

The disadvantages

Apart from the cost, the other 'downside' to in-ear monitors is that they do take a while to adjust to—because everything sounds very different. Because crowd noise is reduced, you can often feel alienated from your audience. To prevent this feeling, a lot of major artist production companies set up crowd microphones so that the crowd can be heard more clearly by the performer. Usually, most performers start by using these monitors in only one ear—until they become more familiar with the different sound.

The other difficulty with using in-ear monitors is that you really need an engineer who knows what he is doing!

Despite some disadvantages, in-ear monitors are a valuable asset, especially if you are touring frequently.

Group singing

I think that group singing is much harder than solo work or choral work. It requires a good ear for harmonies and, more importantly, for *vocal blending*. Vocal blending is something that a lot of solo singers find difficult—and even if you can do it, a good sound is largely determined by the 'colour' of the voices within the group.

I can't hear myself!

A lot of people complain that they cannot hear themselves when singing in a group. It is important to hear yourself, but if you can hear yourself more clearly than the others it is a sure sign that you are not blending with the group.

In a group situation you really have to have 'two separate ears'. What I mean by this is that you need to be able to pick out your voice, but still ensure that it is well blended with the others. Your voice should not be 'sticking out'. Rather, it should be working in harmony to create one sound. You need one ear to listen to what you are doing, and one ear to listen to the overall effect to see if your voice is working with the other voices.

Group monitor mix

In a group situation, your monitor mix might be very similar to what it would be in a lead vocal monitor. For example, apart from the voices of the people in the group, you should hear the lead vocal clearly, and the keyboards and guitar for pitching (although you will probably be pitching off the lead vocal—so let's hope that they can sing in key!). In a larger venue, the 'kick and snare' from the drums might also be important—depending on where you are standing.

After all of this, if you are still have difficulty pitching, cup a hand over one ear. You should now be able to hear your voice more clearly. Another option is to wear one earplug—so that you can hear your voice 'inside' your head.

Making good use of rehearsal

In rehearsal times, I often listen to how the other singers are phrasing their words, and where the breath is taken in a line of a song. This is so I can do the same. This 'tightens-up' the sound. (If we are all doing exactly the same thing it is less likely to sound messy.) A pen and lyric sheet is a good idea in rehearsals to make a note of these sorts of changes, especially if you are learning a lot of songs at once.

Relationships in a group

Who you are working with, and how much you work with them, are also important factors to consider. If you have a good relationship with the other singers, you will be more likely to be honest when something isn't working, and less afraid to experiment. Working with the same people on a frequent basis also means that you learn to understand their voices, as well as how you can enhance the colour of the blend with your own voice. It also is a lot more fun!

Good live work etiquette

Getting to know the sound crew

If you are the solo performer for the gig, make sure you go and introduce yourself to the front-of-house engineer (and to the monitor engineer if there is one). No matter how good you are, these guys are the ones who can make or break your gig—so be nice to them! I often go and say 'hello', and have a quick chat. I appreciate that they work really hard at what they do. No matter how mean or rude someone might be, if you remain polite, grateful, and professional you are more likely to communicate more clearly what you want. If there is a problem, don't be afraid to speak up—but treat the engineers as your peers—because this is what they are.

At the sound check

Give the engineer time to work on getting the sound right. Don't sing two lines of a song and yell out that you are having trouble hearing yourself! Remember that it will take time for the engineer to get the levels right—and your vocal is probably the last thing he is going to work on anyway!

I tend to go through the motions of a sound check (sing a couple of songs with the band) until the engineer 'gives me the nod' to let me know that he is working on my vocal—and then I say what I want. This also gives me a chance to warm up to the performance and get a feel for what is actually going on stage.

Keep in mind that if your voice is not warmed-up, it requires different EQ and volume controls than if your voice is already warmed-up. Sometimes an engineer will wait for your voice to warm up before he starts working on your sound—because he knows that it will change (sometimes dramatically).

When you and your engineer are ready, make sure you sing as if in a performance. Some singers often sing in 'half voice' at a sound check because it's not the 'real thing'. They think that they are saving their voices—or perhaps they just can't be bothered! You are defeating the purpose of the sound check if you are not allowing the engineer to hear the dynamics and personality of your voice.

Finally, remember that it is very frustrating for an engineer to have six musicians all telling him what they want at the same time! Just be patient and let him do his job.

On-sound stage

This is mainly for musicians rather than singers, but I think it is important enough to mention in this section. Make sure that your on-stage sound (what you are hearing in the monitors) is not too loud. If it is too loud, it will bleed off the stage and into the audience, which means that the audience will be hearing what should be for your ears only!

Remember that what you are hearing on stage is a 'you-and-your-rig' mix, not an overall 'even' mix or a true performance mix. It also makes things so loud that it is difficult for the singer to sing without belting it out. (Unless you are Robert Plant, your singer ain't gonna like doing that!)

Buying your own gear

As singers we rarely spend money or take the time to understand our equipment. Sometimes I think we are the envy of the band! The most money that we usually spend is on a microphone and a couple of leads that we roll up at the end of a gig! Meanwhile, the boys carry and load their heavy rigs back into the car! (We are not all like this, but they didn't make up all those singers jokes for nothing!) In addition, most singers are often naturally gifted, and might never even bother to have any singing lessons!

If you are really serious about your job, you will always be finding ways to improve. It's a good idea to invest in a really good microphone that you can use at your gigs. For example an SM58 microphone currently costs about £70 to £100. I like to use my own microphone because I know where it's been, and it is therefore more hygienic. There's nothing worse than breathing over someone else's microphone that smells of cigarette smoke and beer! (Unless you sing at church—then all you have to worry about is bad breath!)

You don't need to spend much when you are starting out, but I think a microphone and a couple of leads are a necessity. You could also invest in a microphone stand and some good custom-made earplugs. If you are singing professionally, you could also think about buying an in-ear monitoring system.

I still spend money on singing lessons, books, and courses—anything that will help me understand what I am doing, and will improve my technique. Oh yeah, and of course I spend money on clothes—this is *very* important indeed!

Chapter 10

Studio work

Roma's first time in a studio at the age of fifteen

Chapter 10
Studio work

Studio work is different

Studio work is very different from live work. There are many things you can do live (including singing flat or sharp, and making mistakes!) that you can't get away with in a studio, because everything is recorded to tape and is heard over and over again! To sing well in a studio setting requires discipline, and a clear understanding of what your voice can and cannot do.

The vocal booth

Let's start with how to use your equipment. In a studio, there is usually a vocal booth and a control room. The control room contains all the equipment needed to record, and is where the engineer works. The vocal booth is where you record vocals and instrumentals. Sometimes there might be more rooms than these—depending on what the studio caters for (orchestra, grand piano, and so on).

Figure 10.1 (page 106) shows a picture of a vocal booth in a studio. As you can see there are a few different elements that work together in a vocal booth. A typical vocal booth contains the following:

- headphone amp;
- pop screen filter;
- studio microphone; and
- acoustic treatment.

Headphone amp

Your headphones are plugged into the headphone amp (see Figure 10.2). It controls how much track and vocal level you want to hear. A headphone amp is particularly good to use when two or more people are singing together—because you can adjust each individual headphone set to suit your ears.

Figure 10.2
Headphone amp

Figure 10.1
Vocal booth at Rick's Place studios, Soho, London (A: headphone amp; B: pop screen filter; C: studio microphone; D: acoustic treatment)

Pop screen filter

The pop screen reduces popping and sibilant sounds (your 'Ps and Qs'). See Figure 10.3. It also allows you to concentrate more on emotion and tone, and enables the engineer to record and edit your vocal more easily. This is especially important when singing solo (rather than in a group vocal session), because you will normally be closer to the microphone in solo work.

Figure 10.3
Pop screen filter

Studio microphone

Depending on the type of voice you have and the style of song you are singing, different microphones are used. Generally, a valve microphone is the most common— because it produces a warm, rich tone (see Figure 10.4). Valve microphones have a large diaphragm, which allows a wider range of frequencies to be recorded. (You can read more about microphones in Chapter 9, 'Live work', page 91.)

Figure 10.4
Studio microphone

Acoustic treatment

The shape and size of the room, and what materials have been used in building it, all affect how things will sound when they have been recorded. This is because sound is reflective. If you have two flat surfaces that are parallel (like walls), and you create sound between these flat surfaces, sound will bounce and create a natural echo or 'reverb'. This can interfere with recording, especially when recording a voice (see Figure.10.5, page 108).

To prevent this problem, acoustic diffusers can be placed in certain sections of the room. If you don't have a lot of money, this can be achieved with egg cartons (available at all good supermarkets!), although most working studios have professional acoustic diffusers. Most singers don't notice this kind of

Figure 10.5
Acoustic treatment prevents echo or 'reverb'

stuff—because it is just part of the room—but next time you're in a studio, have a look around.

How to use your microphone

When recording vocals, the closer you are to a microphone, the warmer your voice will sound. Depending on what style of song you are singing, this can be very important. For example, if you are singing a soft ambient ballad with sparse instrumentation, singing as close to the microphone as possible gives your voice a lot of richness and warmth. If you have a 'toppy', thin voice, the further from the microphone you are, the thinner it will sound.

Your engineer will usually tell you what he or she needs, and can also enhance your vocal sound with good compression, effects, and so on. But it's always advisable to get it right from the beginning.

How to use your headphones

Everyone has his or her own preference regarding the use of headphones. You will have to experiment to find out what works for you. Here are some ideas.

One 'can' on, one 'can' off

If you have one ear covered with a 'can' (one earpiece of a headphone) and the other ear uncovered, you can hear the track and simultaneously hear yourself in the room. Most people prefer this method because they can hear themselves more clearly, and they feel more confident that they are pitching correctly. Again, it really depends on what your personal preferences are.

Hear yourself

Make sure that you can hear yourself! If the track is too loud you are likely to 'push' your singing to hear your voice, and this can lead to your singing sharp. It will eventually lead to vocal fatigue.

Instruments to help you pitch and keep in time

Work out which instruments in the track help you to pitch and keep in time. For example, if it's the piano, and if there are several rhythm guitar tracks that seem to go against the melody or rhythm of the vocal, ask for the guitars to be turned down and for the piano to be turned up. If you have had difficulty hitting notes or keeping time, it could be because you are listening to the wrong things. It's amazing how changing a few levels makes it much easier to vocalise.

Headphones and doubling tracks

When doubling tracks (singing the same line again on another track to create a stereo sound) you might like to have the first double in only one side of your headphones, and what you are actually singing in the other side of your headphones. This assists you to differentiate between what is already on tape and what you are presently doing.

Studio singing

Studio singing vs live singing

Don't sing in the studio what you know that you will have trouble singing live. This is especially important for original music artists. I have done this, and then had to modify live performances.

Something in the studio might sound great at the time, but might feel unnatural and therefore be impossible to produce live. For example, you might find that you are forced to sing too high or too low, and so on.

Group vocals

When singing in a group, it's important that you can hear what and how the others are singing. What is the vocal blend like—soft tone, hard tone, strong tone? How can you blend with the others to get good group sound? Where is everyone taking breaths? Are you ending your notes together? Is your diction too strong or different from the others?

Remember that the microphone picks up everything so the recording has to be near perfect.

Singing and doubling tracks

When you are doubling vocal tracks, don't sing something you know you will have trouble duplicating! From past experience I have done this and, after hours of trying unsuccessfully to recreate it, I have had to go back and change the first track. Keeping it simple is the best way!

Recording a lead vocal 'take'

Everyone has their preferences

Everyone likes to record in different ways. For example, I know engineers who like singers to sing line by line, so that every single note is perfect and so that the emotion they want to project is exactly where they want it. As a vocalist, I find this extremely tiring, stressful, and boring—not to mention unnatural! However, it does depend on the style of music that is being recorded and whether you are doing a session, as opposed to recording original material.

Session music

Singing a session for someone else should be approached very differently from singing your own songs. If you are being employed to do a session, different engineers and producers have different methods for getting the best out of a vocalist.

In this setting, it is a good idea to start off by asking what the engineer, producer, and/or client want from you, and then speaking to them about what makes you comfortable. You will find most people are quite accommodating because they want to get the best out of you.

It is still important to be confident and ask for what you want. You will find that most people will want to do what works best for you because they want a good vocal take! You can be assertive without being bossy.

However, keep in mind that in a session it is difficult to be free in asserting your own personality and style—because this might be distracting. For example, if you are singing for an advertising commercial, it could take the focus off the product being sold and draw attention to the voice. Or if you are singing backing vocals on a track you might sound better than the lead vocalist!

Original music

When singing original music, you have more control over how you can sing. You can also add your own style and personality—after all, this is what original music is all about!

When singing my original material, I often sing through a song once until I am happy with my headphone level, and until the engineer is happy with tone, compression, and so on. Then I sing through the song two or three times. After that I go and sit in the control room with the engineer and piece together the best sections from those few takes. If there is anything that doesn't sound too great, I go back into the vocal booth and re-record that specific line.

I find that this routine reduces vocal fatigue, and that I project more emotion, as it is not becoming too mundane. It is also much quicker to record in this way. When you are singing in studios all the time, it can be difficult to put feeling into a song, so this works best for me. (My attention span is very short!)

'Reverb'

'Reverb' is a sound effect that is most commonly used on the voice. It basically makes the voice sound 'wet' —rather than sounding dry and stark.

Sometimes having a little reverb on your vocal can help you sing better. It really depends on the song and how you are required to sing. For example, if you are required to sing soft and high, you might find that reverb helps you to sing a little more lightly and helps you not to force your tone.

However, reverb can make you sing flat or sharp—because it changes what you are hearing in your headphones. Singing dry (without any effect on your voice) does give the best indication of what is actually being recorded—but find out what works best for you.

Clearing your throat and not warming up

As a session is progressing, it is quite common to observe a vocalist repeatedly clearing his or her throat, or repeatedly warming-up.

Warming-up is imperative before you begin. This is because everything about your voice changes as it warms up—from frequencies to clarity of tone. This is more noticeable when you are recording. Over several takes, your voice can sound vastly different—thus creating more work for the engineer, and for you.

Clearing the throat is damaging, and is usually a nervous reaction. It is usually unnecessary. One of the dangers of not warming-up, and of repeatedly clearing your throat, is increased vocal fatigue. In a studio situation, vocal fatigue is far more obvious than when singing live. This means that with every take it becomes more noticeable that the quality and sound of your voice is changing. With some voices this can be quite dramatic.

Clothes or jewellery

Don't wear noisy clothes or jewellery, and so on. The microphone picks up everything! This piece of advice might sound unimportant, but you use your body a lot when you are singing (I use my hands all the time!), and unwanted noise from such things as clothes and jewellery can be a real problem.

Relax

Enjoy yourself! Remember that you are singing because you love it. So relax, and give your best performance!

Chapter 11

Choral work

Melbourne Gospel Choir at Carols by Candlelight (GTV9), 2000, Melbourne

Chapter 11
Choral work

A team effort

In this chapter we will talk about how to be an effective choir member, an effective choir director, how to learn and teach harmonies, and how to conduct a choir.

Singing in a choir is one of the best ways to develop an ear for harmonies and blending, and for working with people. When I was growing up, I worked in *a cappella* groups and choirs, and I now have the pleasure of coordinating the Melbourne Gospel Choir, which does most of its work on television. It's so different from solo work! In fact, I think that group singing and choral work are much harder than solo work—because it requires a team effort.

The choir member
Warm up before you arrive

Rehearsals are for learning songs—not for maintaining your voice. Save time and vocal strain by coming already warmed-up.

Warming-up in advance also changes the 'colour' and frequencies of your voice—which is very important for blending with others. So come ready!

Turn up on time

I think this speaks for itself! Group activity depends on group cooperation. Being on time is a matter of courtesy.

Bring a bottle of water with you

Always bring a bottle of water with you. You need this to keep your throat hydrated and to combat vocal fatigue. Long rehearsals can be tiring.

Bring a portable tape recorder

A portable tape recorder is useful so you can record your parts and take them home to learn. This is an extremely valuable tool for working singers.

Lyric sheet and notepaper

If a lyric sheet is provided, write yourself notes. Take notes on anything you must remember to do. For example, you can underline where you need to come in. You will be surprised how quickly you forget things when you walk away from the rehearsal!

Vocal blending

Learn to listen to the other voices in your group, and adapt your voice accordingly. For example, if everyone is singing 'breathy' and soft, don't 'belt'— you will just stand out. Remember that a choir is about being one unit. Where is everyone taking breaths? What are the vocal dynamics? Are you singing flat or sharp?

Vocal harmonies

Learn the melody first

Learn the melody first until you are confident. Learning harmonies becomes much easier when you have a grasp of the melody.

Think in pictures

If you think in pictures you might find grasping harmonies a little easier. For example, listen to the rise and fall of the notes and draw a line in your head (or on paper), that follows the progression of the notes.

Some people are naturals at picking up harmonies; others find it more difficult. A choir is the perfect place to develop a discipline in this area. But don't put everyone else off in the process! (See Chapter 7, 'Placement imagery', for more on this subject.)

Listen to a lot of music

If you want to improve your skill at singing parts, listen to a lot of music. Instead of listening to the lead vocal, or the main instrumentation, see what else you can hear. Are there any other voices singing? Is it different from the lead vocal? Try to listen for things you would not normally listen for. Sing along to the backing vocals! You will be surprised at how much you can learn, and you will gain a deeper appreciation for song structure and arrangement.

Gain an understanding of chord structure

Gain an understanding of chord structure. Piano or theory lessons can make a huge difference to your skills in musicianship. You will find that your skill for harmonies will improve, and that you will become a more confident musician.

Don't assume what your part is

Many singers assume what their parts are—especially when they sing harmonies all the time. There is often more than one way to sing a part—so be careful, and listen to what is being directed, rather than singing what is most natural or common for you.

Don't sing another part because you think it's better

Don't sing another part because you think it's better. Remember that your part needs to work with all the other sections of the choir, and you need to follow what is happening. Yes, your idea may be great. Indeed, it might even sound better than what the choir director has suggested. But you are not the director! Don't make it hard for the director by not working with the rest of the team.

Don't talk all the time

It's noisy when everyone talks all the time. This is tiring for all concerned, and you won't hear when instructions are given.

People talking all the time is really annoying for the director. It means that they have to repeat instructions for those who haven't listened. If there are fifty people in the group and half of them ask for a repeat of instructions which have already been given, the director becomes understandably annoyed. It is extremely disruptive and unprofessional.

Even if you are not working in a professional choir, remember you will never move to bigger and better things if you don't have a professional attitude from the beginning.

The choir director

Designate team leaders

Team leaders can be appointed to take a section of the choir and teach these people their individual parts. A leader can make sure that the team (or subgroup) is working effectively, both musically and personally.

I have found this to be an effective way of spreading out the workload. And it also develops the skills and talents of the appointed leaders. If a director is prepared to delegate responsibility in this way, it is a sign of good leadership. Instead of being threatened, you are developing others to be leaders as well.

When I coordinate the Melbourne Gospel Choir for television performances, I know that I can't do it effectively on my own. The job is huge. As the director, I must liaise with television personnel, and make sure that the artist, the band, and the camera crew are all happy. On top of this, I need to make sure that the choir learns the parts (which I must know inside out), and that they all turn up on time to rehearsals and to the gig. And through it all, I must have a good attitude! I simply can't do all of those things effectively without the help of my team leaders. (Rebecca Watkins and Esther Oakley you're the best!). Breaking up the team into smaller groups makes it much easier to handle, and also allows me to concentrate on how the choir looks and sounds as a whole. I wouldn't know what I would do without my team leaders. They have become the backbone of the choir.

Choosing team leaders

When choosing team leaders, it is important to ensure that the people who are chosen have a mixture of sound musical knowledge and good people skills. They don't necessarily need to be able to read music, but they should have a good ear for harmonies and be able to communicate this well to their subgroups.

Your team leaders should also respect and support your decisions as the director (even if they don't agree with them), and should feel that they can be open with you about what is working, and what is not working. They need to be assertive, but not too strong. They need to love people!

Write simple parts

You might think that writing complicated parts will make you all sound amazing. However, the truth is that with a large group of singers, the simpler the parts the better!

There are several reasons for this.

1. The more complicated the parts, the harder it is for the group to learn. And the bigger the group, the bigger the train crash! One little mistake (perhaps just one note) sounds absolutely terrible when fifty people make it! If you want your choir to sound amazing, keep it simple.

2. It is your job to make sure the choir sounds great as a whole. But with complex parts, you can find it difficult to hear if one section is making small mistakes. If you create 'block' harmonies that are easy to follow, the choir can almost take care of itself.

3. If the parts are easy to grasp, the choir is more confident. It is better to have a confident choir singing simple parts, than a nervous choir singing complicated parts.

4. Remember that singing great is only half the battle. The choir needs to look great. It's very easy to get so caught up in how everyone sounds, and then, at the last minute, find that you have to work on getting everyone to smile and learn some simple moves (if required). Often this sort of thing is left to the last minute—because too much time has been spent working out complicated parts (most of which are usually discarded for simpler parts anyway). Most of the time I do only simple three-part harmonies, or four-parts in some sections. Because of the number of people singing, it always sounds great.

Be a leader and not a dictator

Make sure that you are not on a power trip! There are plenty of people in the Melbourne Gospel Choir who could effectively do my job—because a majority of them are professional singers in their own right. It is a privilege to have the people you have in your choir, and a privilege to serve them with good leadership.

Because you happen to have a position of authority, don't dictate to other people, or put them down. It makes people feel worthless, and eventually they won't want to work with you.

Our choir works well because we are all having fun and genuinely care about each other. If you are too overpowering, you could destroy that.

Don't take things too personally

The more people you have in your group, the more opinions you will have to deal with. There have been times when I have been conducting a rehearsal, and have had so many people telling me what to do, that I forgot just what my own suggestion was in the first place!

Take the attitude that, in a room full of singers (and egos!), there will be plenty of people who could do your job. Some of them might even do it better than you. But the fact is that you are the leader, so make the rules the best way you know how. And don't take it too personally when people challenge your authority. If you are good at what you do, you will stand the test of time. As they say, 'the proof of the pudding is in the eating'—so be confident that you can do the job and that you can rise to the occasion, without getting too emotional about it all.

How to teach parts

There are several ways you can teach parts. Here are a couple of methods I have used that have worked well. What you choose will depend on the style of music you are singing, the musicianship of the choir, and how much time you have to learn a choral piece.

Teach the melody first

Harmonies are much easier to learn when the melody has been solidified. Start your rehearsal by teaching the melody. Once the choir is confident, separate into parts.

Record the parts onto a tape

If you don't read music, or if you have no sheet music to follow, record each part onto a tape. This is to ensure that they all work first!

I have a small home studio and I record all the parts together. Then I record them onto a tape separately for each specific group. This is a good method, because you can post tapes to all choir members before your first rehearsal and everyone comes along knowing what he or she is meant to be singing. It's more preparation for you, but less work and time is spent at rehearsals sorting stuff out.

Write out the parts or have the sheet music

If you can write and read music, this is the best way to teach parts. However, if most of your choir members are not good sight-readers, they will still lack confidence. Personally, I like to have the sheet music in front of me to read, but I have found that most choral singers tend to learn more slowly this way. It really depends on the musicianship and style of the choir.

If you do use sheet music, don't become so technical that you lose feeling and dynamics. Be sensitive to the song and what the other singers are doing.

Have a rehearsal with your team leaders

Sometimes I get together with my team leaders and we work out the parts together. Basically it's like a mini-rehearsal with three or four people. We work on our own harmonies, sing them together, and see what works. Then we put them onto a tape.

When choir rehearsal comes, the team leaders can take their groups away to learn their sections. This is an extremely effective way of conducting a productive rehearsal.

However, if you are a 'control freak', this method will not work!

How to conduct a choir

Be very visual if the parts are difficult

I often use my hands and face to direct. The more excited you look, the more the choir will feed off your enthusiasm. In fact, if you want to see the choir advance musically and visually, you have to step out even further than they do. One step for them means ten steps for you! It's hard work, but it works.

Use hand signals and body language

Hand signals and body language are very important. For example, when the notes are going up or down, use your hands to indicate this. Work out signals that require choir members to end or hold their notes.

You are the person to whom they look to make them sound like one unit—so be definite and confident with your body language. Let them know when they are required to move by moving yourself.

And smile at them—it's infectious!

Chapter 12
Touring and gigging

Chapter 12
Touring and gigging

How to look after yourself on the road

Few people understand the pressures of touring. Most people consider travelling to be exciting and fun, but if you are doing it all the time it can become extremely tiring and stressful. Of course, you would never give it up for anything else, but if precautions aren't set in place to take care of yourself, the candle burns brightly from both ends, very quickly, until you're left wondering why you thought it was so great in the first place!

The 'rulebook' of the music industry is to live 'fast and hard'. But the truth is that you can't do this forever and expect your body to remain healthy. 'Balance' is a word that every creative person hates—but balance pays off in the end.

I have a love/hate relationship with touring. If you do a lot of travelling yourself, I'm sure you understand what I mean. In this chapter I share some of the secrets that have helped me to stay on top of things.

Jetlag
Living life on a plane

'Jetlag' is *not* my favourite word! I think the biggest number of flights that I have made in one batch consisted of ten flights in twelve days. Every day, except for one, was a gig. In addition, there were radio and magazine interviews, in-store appearances, and so on. Luckily they were short trips—but nevertheless I experienced jetlag, especially when I arrived back home. I remember that I had to go straight from the plane to a rehearsal!

What is jetlag?

The symptoms of jetlag include feelings of extreme tiredness, lack of concentration, lack of motivation, irritability, irrationality, and haziness. Some people also experience broken sleep—especially after they return from a trip.

Other effects of jetlag can include poor circulation (which can lead to limb swelling), headaches, nasal irritation, dry skin, diarrhoea, and dehydration. It can also reduce your resistance to colds and 'flu.

Jetlag is caused by a number of factors—including crossing time zones (messing up your body's time clock and rhythms) and dehydration due to the dry atmosphere in the aircraft. Being overtired or stressed, or having a hangover or the 'flu before you leave, can also increase the effects of jetlag.

How do I prevent or reduce it?

Rest

People often say that they will catch up on their sleep once they get on the plane—but this is probably the worst thing that you can do. (I know this from personal experience!) A good night's rest before you travel extensively is really beneficial and practical.

Sleeping pills and plane travel don't mix. Take them only if you really have to do so. Because sleeping tablets encourage a 'comatose' state, there is little or no body movement. This encourages poor circulation, which can enhance the potential for blood clotting. Some sleeping tablets are also variants of anti-histamines, and this can increase dehydration.

Oops! Overslept!

I know a story of a lady who was leaving Europe to fly back to Australia. This lady 'popped' a few sleeping pills before the plane actually took off.

Unfortunately, there were mechanical complications with the plane. After some time waiting for take-off, all passengers were asked to exit the plane and wait for another flight.

The sleeping tablets had already taken effect, and the poor lady had to be carried off to wait for another flight!

Keep well hydrated

Drink lots and lots of water. Cabin pressure and 'stale' air increase the risk of dehydration. Don't drink a lot of alcohol, tea, or coffee if you want to stay well hydrated. Apart from the fact that these substances have a dehydrating effect on your body, the effects of alcohol are increased while flying. One glass of wine in the air is equivalent to two or three glasses on the ground. In addition, the coffee and tea on some airlines has higher levels of caffeine (although some of you might like that!).

If you are travelling extensively (especially overseas), purified (distilled) water is great because there are no chemicals in it that could introduce more impurities to your body.

Saline nasal spray is also very good if you find that your nasal passages become very dry and sore when on a long flight.

Exercise

The day before travelling, I recommend some form of exercise to increase your body's circulation. This is really just commonsense—you are going to be sitting down for hours, so get your blood flowing beforehand as much as possible.

While you are on the plane, get up every hour or so to stretch your legs. Walk up and down the aisle. Do some stretches and take in some really good breaths. I find that taking my shoes off is also a good idea (although there are some people who argue with that advice).

Ask for an aisle seat when you book your flight. This allows you to move about the cabin without disturbing other passengers. If I am on a particularly long flight, I ask for an exit row because there is more leg room.

Sleeping aids

Sleeping aids can improve your resting time on the plane—blindfolds, earplugs, blankets, some good CDs, and so on are all useful.

Diet

Be practical. Don't eat a huge fatty meal when you know you are going to have to sit for ten hours. In fact, don't even eat the plane food if you are not hungry. Fresh fruit and vegetables are always good. For more information on good dietary practice, see Chapter 15, 'You are what you eat', page 161.

Coping through time zones

When flying, it is a good idea to get up and catch the sun in the mornings when you are about to arrive at your destination. This can help your internal time clock to adjust. (Unfortunately if you are doing gigs at the North Pole this will be a problem!)

If you are arriving at your destination during the day, resist the temptation to have a sleep. Try to wait until bedtime at your point of arrival.

Natural therapies

Homoeopathic and other herbal medicines are beneficial. I have found that chamomile tea can reduce sleeplessness, impatience, and stress. Other options include Bach flower remedies such as olive—which are available at most health food shops.

Seek the advice of a professional before taking any form of medication so they can advise what would be best for you.

What about melatonin?

There has been much talk about melatonin being useful in combating jetlag. Melatonin is a natural hormone secreted by the pineal gland in the brain. This hormone is secreted when the day becomes dark. It helps to regulate our sleep/wake cycles, and therefore encourages sleep. It might therefore be useful for jetlag. Many people who travel extensively have used it with great results, although there are still concerns about its side-effects.

As yet, there is not enough evidence to prove whether melatonin is effective. The short-term effects seem to be beneficial, but long-term effects have yet to be determined. Some negative side-effects of taking melatonin include headaches, nightmares, grogginess in the mornings, and depression. It should also be noted that it can be difficult to take. For example, if you don't take it at exactly the right times, it might actually increase the effects of jetlag.

In some countries, melatonin can be obtained only on a prescription, although it is available in the United States over the counter. I advise you to talk with your health practitioner to see if it is a viable option for you.

Motion sickness

If you experience serious motion sickness, 'acu-pressure' wristbands with a half-ball or node in the middle of each band can be beneficial. They strap around the wrist and prevent motion sickness in some people on take-off and landing. You can ask for them at any chemist. (However, once I became used to travelling I didn't need them any more.)

Sucking on a piece of ginger can also be helpful for alleviating motion sickness in some people.

Earplugs

Your ears are a great asset!

As a singer, your ears are one of your greatest assets—so it is important to look after them. Exposure to high levels of noise can result in tinnitus (ringing in the ears) and other significant problems. One of the best investments I have made was to purchase some professional custom-made earplugs.

What are custom-made earplugs?

Industrial earplugs, such as the ones you buy at the chemist, cut out a majority of surrounding noise—especially higher frequencies. This is insufficient for musicians and singers who need to hear what is going on when performing.

Custom-made earplugs, which are made from an impression of your ear canal so they fit perfectly, do not block out all sound completely. But they do reduce the sound to a safer level. With such custom-made earplugs you can request how much protection you want. For example, you can request 10dB protection, 15dB protection, or 20dB protection—depending on what you require them for.

When having your earplugs fitted, you will normally have a hearing test done as well.

How do I use them?

Some performers use these earplugs comfortably when they are singing solo, and they can also be used when singing backing vocals—although it can take a while to get used to hearing things differently.

A common use for these earplugs is to wear them in between sets or at someone else's gig. I have found that when the music is really loud and I am trying to have a conversation with someone, I tend to yell to be heard. After a couple of hours of doing this I experience vocal fatigue. When I wear custom-made earplugs it is, in fact, *easier* to hear other people, and I can hear myself more clearly. I can feel and hear the sensation of my voice in my face and head, and this makes me speak at a safer level.

I do this all the time now and I don't have to suffer the consequences of a tired voice (or tired ears!) the next day. As I mentioned, as a singer, your ears are one of your greatest assets. Look after them!

Sleeping on the road

Sleeping tablets

I find it very difficult to sleep on the road. Sleeping tablets can be good if you don't have to get up early the next day. They can also be beneficial if you are travelling through different time zones. I sometimes use them on the first night of arrival at my new destination.

Natural remedies

Although sleeping tablets have their uses, natural remedies are preferable. There are heaps of these, but some of the most commonly used include valerian, certain teas (such as chamomile), and other various relaxing herbal remedies.

A few drops of lavender massaged into your temples and the middle of your forehead just before you go to bed is quite relaxing. Or you might like to try a bath salts and lavender bath (see box, below).

Bath salts and lavender

If you have the luxury of a bath before you go to bed, this little remedy works wonders:

- a handful of bath salts;
- ten drops of lavender oil.

  Add bath salts and lavender oil to a warm bath.

  Relax and enjoy!

Standard earplugs

Standard soft earplugs, available at chemists, are great as well—especially if you are sleeping in someone's house, rather than in a hotel. Friends are very kind to give you accommodation, but with lots of kids who get up and have showers at 6 am ... do I sound bitter?

Deep breathing

Deep-breathing exercises can make a huge difference to sleeping patterns. You might like to try the breathing exercise that I often use (see box, page 132).

An excellent breathing technique is the Middendorf method. This is not only great for relaxation, but also very good for strengthening breath-support for singing. It is taught in the UK by several singing teachers, and there are webpages on the Internet if you would like more information.

Breathing relaxation exercise

1. Get into bed and stretch out. Have a big yawn.

2. Lying on your back, take a deep breath, allowing your diaphragm and lungs to expand slowly. Do not let your shoulders rise.

3. Once you have filled up your lungs to a comfortable level, exhale. Do not do this too quickly or too slowly. Exhale as you would if you were sighing or yawning.

4. Allow your body to do nothing for a moment. See if you can do nothing for about five to ten seconds.

5. Take in another breath and repeat the exercise until you feel relaxed.

Vitamins and minerals on the road

If you are travelling frequently, I strongly recommend taking some vitamin and mineral supplements. Even if you do take precautions with your eating and sleeping habits it is easy to become run down. Your health practitioner can advise regarding what is right for you.

Vocal warm-ups on the road

Like an athlete in training

Warming-up on the road, or during a period in which you are doing a lot of singing work, should be significantly different from what you do in your normal day-to-day singing routine. An athlete training for the Olympics can spend five hours a day or more exercising to increase stamina, endurance, and strength. However, during the Olympics, that athlete needs to conserve energy for the event, and training time is therefore significantly reduced during those days. Athletes call this 'tapering'.

I do not recommend that you practise for five hours a day like an athlete! But, like an athlete striving to improve performance in preparation for a big event, you should always be trying to improve your voice and should strive to keep it in good working order during the course of your singing practice. And, just as an athlete 'tapers' as the big event is due, during a tour or a long series of concerts, your practice time should be reduced. If you are physically tired you will find it increasingly difficult to support your voice with correct breathing and resonance. This can make your voice tired, and vocal fatigue during a tour is not what you want!

Cutting down the load

When I have a lot of work on, I cut down my practice time and make it into 'maintenance time'. I warm up my voice completely, and rely on the practice time I have had prior to the concerts to keep my voice on track.

In addition, I don't warm up immediately before a show. This would mean that I would be singing for hours without a break—which is a sure way to experience vocal fatigue! I warm up a couple of hours before a show, and then have a break for dinner, or a shower, or whatever. Then, before my performance, I do a couple of quick vocal scales before I go on stage. This normally takes five to ten minutes. I also do a lot of body stretching to relax.

Get advice

If you have a singing teacher, he or she should be able to help you with a program to use when you are travelling.

I also take several tapes of singing lessons with me. These tapes are of sessions that I have had with my teacher at various stages in my vocal training. For example, if I have had the 'flu, I have lessons on tape which were recorded just after I had the 'flu at some other time. I also have tapes that feel like a real workout, and other tapes that are more for maintenance (rather than learning something new).

Chapter 13

Singing while playing an instrument

Carolyn Oates, Acoustic Cafe tour 1996

PUBLISHED WITH PERMISSION OF STEVE FILBY

Roma Waterman, Acoustic Cafe tour 1996

Chapter 13
Singing while playing an instrument

Easy to strain your voice

Singing while playing an instrument, and doing so without straining your voice, can be difficult. It is very easy to fall into bad habits. Changing some simple things about your posture while sitting or standing will make a significant difference to your voice. You can do these things without changing your own individual style.

Guitarists and bass players
Position of the microphone

One of the major things to concentrate on is the position of the microphone in relation to your posture. For example, guitarists can find that they naturally tend to sing with their necks protruding forward and the rest of their bodies away from the microphone, causing their spines to be out of alignment. This makes it difficult to breathe properly, and also causes tension in their throats.

If you find that you do this, practise changing the position of your body so that you don't do these things. What feels comfortable? Are you able to breathe more freely? Do you experience less tension?

Your microphone stand

What sort of microphone stand are you using? Is it an upright microphone (completely straight) or is it a boomstand (a movable arm)? This might sound a stupid question, but it makes a difference to how you stand when you sing. An upright stand is normally used only for singing—not for playing and singing. This is because an upright does not allow a lot of room between the stand and the instrument. This means that you are more likely to step back to make room, but stick your neck forward so that your mouth is closer to the microphone. Clearly a boomstand is the more obvious choice in this situation.

Position your boomstand further away from you, increase the height of the boom, and then bring the arm down towards your mouth. This way you can be as close to the microphone as you wish, without the base of the stand getting in the way.

How you wear your guitar or bass

People who wear their instruments quite low tend to hunch their shoulders forwards. You can still carry your instrument the way you want, just be aware of what it does to your body, and rectify the problems accordingly.

Drummers

Hard work

I think this is the hardest instrument to combine with your voice. You're usually sitting on a low stool, and there is a lot of movement required from your upper body. Add singing to this and it becomes really hard work! On top of this, you have to keep the rest of the band in time!

How you sit

Note how you sit on your stool and what effect this has on your breathing. Try sitting so that the base of your spine is taking the weight of your upper body. You should feel that you are sitting on the edge of your seat. Notice that this naturally lifts your upper body because it is difficult to slouch in this position.

If you're the type of drummer who likes to sink into the whole seat, try to sit as straight as you can, without arching your back. It is difficult to do if you like to sink into the whole seat, but in time it becomes easier—so give it a go!

I think that a headset microphone is the best option for singing drummers. This way you won't need to be conscious of leaning forwards—which naturally restricts upper body movement.

If you do use an upright stand, have it positioned with the microphone coming down from above on an angle—which will position the microphone right on your mouth.

Piano players

Standing

If you stand and play, are you hunching forward? Don't lean towards the microphone. (By now you are rightly assuming that this is the biggest problem for singing 'musos'!). Is your keyboard stand too low (in which case you will lean forwards), or perhaps too high?

You might find that what 'comes naturally', comes naturally only because you haven't tried any other way! Make some changes and see if it makes a difference to your singing.

Sitting

If you are sitting low, the mid section of your body will be restricted to smaller breaths. Just like drummers, you need to sit so that the base of your spine is supporting your upper body. This might require you to sit closer to the edge of your seat. If your spine is aligned, you will find it easier to breathe, and sitting like this will immediately open up your chest area.

Again, don't hunch forward, and don't lean towards a microphone. I position the microphone right under my mouth, and move back (for dynamics) only when I have to.

PART III

MAINTENANCE

Chapter 14

Voice problems

Chapter 14
Voice problems

Take care

Voice problems are, of course, a constant threat to working singers. This chapter by no means covers all vocal problems that can occur. Rather, I talk about those that are most common for singers and entertainers. Take care of your voice. It is obviously essential to your working career.

In this chapter, we will talk about some common problems encountered by singers. These include:

- nodules;
- smoking;
- alcohol;
- upper respiratory tract infections;
- temporo-mandibular joint disorder;
- tinnitus; and
- dry mouth.

Nodules

Nodules are formed by vocal abuse. Ultimately, the real cure for them is to change the way you sing.

The signs and symptoms

If you have nodules you might be experiencing frequent hoarseness or a very 'breathy' or husky voice—especially in the middle register. You might find it difficult to sing in your upper register, especially softly, and over time you will need to exert more pressure to sustain vocal tone. An increasing difficulty in producing vocal tone can indicate nodules.

Basically, nodules mean that you have to work a lot harder to create sound. Unfortunately, the harder you work, the worse it gets! Keep in mind that you might not be experiencing any pain at all. After all, if you did feel pain, you wouldn't do it!

> **Important to get expert advice**
>
> In reading this chapter on voice problems, please remember that if you are experiencing any vocal difficulty, it is extremely important that a voice specialist properly assesses you.
>
> Do *not* diagnose yourself. And do *not* wait until it's too late.

So what are they?

Nodules are formed on your vocal folds when there is abnormal tension or force being used in singing and/or speaking. The surfaces of normal vocal folds are smooth so they can vibrate easily. When there is too much pressure on these folds, a haematoma (that is, a bruise) develops. Eventually, after constant strain, fibrous tissue replaces the haematoma, becomes larger, and then appears as a white nodule, which can be hard or soft (see Figure 14.1, below).

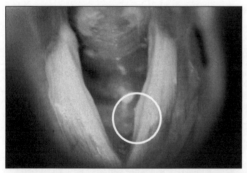

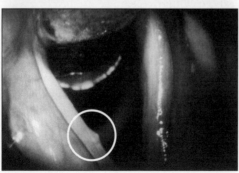

Figure 14.1
Vocal folds with nodules as marked.
PUBLISHED WITH PERMISSION OF ROYAL EYE
AND EAR HOSPITAL, MELBOURNE

I compare the development of nodules with learning to play a guitar. Initially, pressing the strings with your fingers causes a little pain and discomfort. However, as you continue to practise, the tips of your fingers develop a callus in the skin to adapt to the pressure. This is great for guitarists' fingers, but not so great for singers' vocal folds!

Some singers like the sound that nodules produce, and it is common for most vocalists in the pop and rock scene to have nodules and not be bothered by them. However, over time, it will it become increasingly difficult to sing. I know people who cannot sing the way they did five years ago. They are constantly plagued by vocal problems. If you want to have a lifetime career in singing, it is imperative to change these functional problems as soon as possible.

How should I manage my nodules?

No longer surgery for most

Years ago, most doctors suggested surgical removal. Thank goodness times have changed! Now, only in severe cases is surgery considered to be appropriate— and even then laser surgery is used. (This is especially if the nodules are red, rather than white; red nodules indicating more severe damage.)

Voice therapy

The most common form of treatment today is to have about three months or more of voice therapy and modification in the use of your voice. Doctors no longer recommend complete vocal rest. This is because nodules are generally a functional problem, which means it is important that you are taught how to rectify your technique as soon as possible.

For me, voice therapy was extremely effective. It definitely takes a lot of discipline, but when you experience how easy it is to sing clear notes with volume in the right way, you'll never want to go back to the wrong way again. It took about six months for my nodule to disappear, and about a year for me to learn how to maintain my voice correctly.

Some practical guidelines in voice therapy

You will need a teacher to guide you to make sure that you are using your voice correctly. Again, I must stress the importance of seeing a laryngologist to diagnose your situation properly.

Here is a list of things you can do immediately if you have nodules.

When you sing

- Always warm up before you sing (including at rehearsals!).

- Relax your lower jaw, mouth, tongue, and soft palate to reduce muscle tension.

- Don't sing out of your range. Sing where you are comfortable.

- Stay away from dusty and smoky environments. If I know that I will be singing in this sort of environment, I ask people not to smoke backstage, and I ask the lighting guy not to go too crazy on the smoke machine (so I don't choke to death!). Some smoke machines have aloe vera included in their ingredients to make the smoke less harsh on the throat.

- Don't yell over the music in between sets. In fact, most singers lose their voices in this way—rather than singing at the gig!

When you speak

- Pay close attention to your speaking voice. Try to speak above the 'croak'.

- Keep your voice light, but not 'breathy'.

- Breathe well!

Taking vitamin E

Vitamin E is a powerful nutrient in repairing body tissue. Speak to a health practitioner about finding a product that contains the four vitamin E components mentioned below, as well as essential fatty acids (which are powerful antioxidants). Note that not all vitamin E products on the market include these fatty acids.

The four vitamin E components are:

- D-alpha-tocopherol;

- mixed tocopherols;

- selenomethionine; and

- equiv. selenium.

Some other tips

- Stay well hydrated; drink lots of water.

- Regular rest and relaxation and a good diet are essential.

- Get singing lessons and/or speech therapy from a teacher who understands how to get your voice back into peak condition.

- Get regular check-ups with a voice specialist. Having a check-up every 6–12 months will ensure that you keep an eye on things before they get out of hand.

Smoking

Some people can smoke for years without experiencing any vocal difficulty until later in life. Others can't even smoke passively without developing throat problems.

Nevertheless, smoking certainly dehydrates your vocal folds, and the deposits of tar on your lungs causes damage to the lung tissue and cuts down oxygen absorption—which results in shortness of breath. You will also find over time that it leads to problems in obtaining a good vocal tone—especially in your higher register.

Unfortunately, if you decide to give it up, you might find that your voice feels even worse for a while. This is your body adjusting to the change. That's why it's best not to stop while you are working. However, when you have made the decision, do persist. After about six weeks you will notice a significant difference in the clarity of your voice and the ease of singing.

Alcohol

Alcohol has a dehydrating effect on your body. And drinking alcohol increases your body temperature—which means increased blood flow to your vocal folds. This thickens the folds so that when they come together for phonation, they do not come together correctly. You might produce a huskier tone than normal. Needless to say, this also increases throat tension as you need to work harder to produce a clear sound.

Apart from these problems, if you're drunk, you're more likely to make a complete idiot of yourself! Professional behaviour is important in professional singers.

Upper respiratory tract infections (URTIs)

The term 'upper respiratory tract infection' (URTI) refers to laryngitis, pharyngitis, coughs, colds, and so on.

Laryngitis

Laryngitis is an inflammation of the vocal folds to the point of partial or complete vocal loss. It can be bacterial or viral in origin, or it might result from overusing your voice (such as at a football match!).

When your folds are inflamed, phonation becomes a problem, resulting in hoarseness and deterioration in the quality of sound. So if it hurts in your throat when you swallow do *not* attempt to sing.

Pharyngitis

Pharyngitis is an inflammation of the oral and nasal pharynx—the part of the vocal tract just above the larynx (or voice box). The oral pharynx extends up to the soft palate. The nasal pharynx extends up into the nose. You can see part of the pharynx if you look into a mirror, open wide and say 'ah'. The soft palate will lift to show part of the pharynx.

Dangers of URTIs

If you persist in singing when you have an URTI, you can cause unnecessary damage to your throat, and perhaps to your vocal folds. Pharyngitis can easily develop into laryngitis. In addition, you might develop nodules during an URTI, and you can develop prolonged huskiness of voice if you don't take time to rest and allow your body to recover.

Treatments for URTIs

They say that there is no cure for the 'common cold', but there are various things that you can do to help you get over an URTI more quickly. Some treatments for URTIs include the following.

Antibiotics

Antibiotics might be prescribed for your URTI if it is a bacterial infection.

Rest

Rest in general is a good idea if you are feeling unwell. In particular, lots of vocal rest is essential.

Hydration and vaporisation

Keep your body and your vocal folds well hydrated by drinking lots of fluids. And vaporising is really good for hydrating the folds. Place your head over a bowl of very hot water, with a towel over your head, and inhale until the steam is gone. You can add a few drops of tea-tree oil, or lemon oil; both have antibacterial properties.

Echinacea, horseradish, and garlic

Although echinacea, horseradish, and garlic have excellent antibacterial properties, if you are going to sing don't take huge doses of anything that clears up mucus. This has a drying effect on your vocal folds. Your folds need moisture to function properly. I do take echinacea when I am not well, but I do not take large amounts if I have numerous singing engagements.

Throat lozenges

Anti-inflammatory throat lozenges can be helpful. And some of them have a mild anaesthetic effect which numbs the throat slightly. However, be careful not to take them if you intend to sing because you will be unaware of how much you are 'pushing' your voice. This, in turn, can lead to further difficulties down the track.

Throat gargles

There are several throat gargles on the market for throat and mouth infections.

If you prefer to use a home-made throat gargle, try the one described in the box (below).

Natural honey

Natural honey is really amazing—especially for reducing coughing spasms. I recently had bronchitis and took a tablespoon of honey every hour or so. It significantly reduced the amount of coughing I suffered.

Honey is safe and is known to have a healing ability. It has antibacterial properties, and can break down the mucus that causes congestion. Tea-tree or manuka honey is especially high in antibacterial agents. Honey and lemon mixed with hot water makes a soothing drink. It tastes nice too!

Home-made throat gargle mixture

This was given to me by my naturopath. You will find it extremely effective:

- 1 teaspoon of sea salt
- 1 teaspoon bicarbonate of soda
- a few drops of tea-tree oil
- warm water

Mix all the ingredients together and gargle as often as needed.

Do not swallow.

(PS It tastes disgusting!)

Changing your performance schedule

Modify your performances, and perhaps shorten them if you have to. However, keep in mind that the best solution for a major illness is to shut up completely, and rest—or you could be in real trouble!

Sinus trouble remedies

Sometimes an URTI can develop into a significant congestion and stuffiness in the sinuses. There are some great concoctions on the market for sinus trouble. For example, 'Nasaya Herbal', available from your naturopath, is very good.

If you prefer to prepare your own home remedy, try the sinus home remedy described in the box (below).

Home-made sinus remedy

This was given to me by my naturopath. You will find it extremely effective:

Ingredients

- 1 bottle of Swedish bitters (Swedish bitters break down the build-up of mucus in the sinuses; they can be purchased from a health food shop or from large supermarkets)
- cottonwool strips

Method

1. Soak the cottonwool strips in Swedish bitters.

2. Lie down and place the cottonwool strips on the affected sinus areas. You can also put some cottonwool inside your nose if you are really suffering.

3. Leave in position for an hour or so. Read a good book (such as this one) while you are at it!

Temporo-mandibular joint (TMJ) disorder

What is it?

On each side of your face, a temporo-mandibular joint (TMJ) connects your lower jaw (mandible) to the temple bone of your skull. Inflammation in this joint can cause a lot of pain in your face and jaw, and sometimes in your neck. This is known as temporo-mandibular joint disorder (TMJ disorder).

Symptoms can include a dull ache in your lower jaw and skull, and difficulty in opening and closing your mouth. 'Popping' of the jaw and headaches are also common. Some sufferers of TMJ disorder even find it difficult to chew crunchy foods without their jaw 'clicking' and causing severe pain.

My own experience

I have suffered from TMJ disorder for many years. However, as a result of the various treatments mentioned below, I have been able to reduce the pain and other problems significantly.

There were times when I used to wake up in the morning with my jaw so stiff that I could not open my mouth! Needless to say, to get it 'back into position' was very painful. I would sometimes have to punch myself, and my jaw and the back of my neck would hurt for days afterwards.

When performing, there have been times when my jaw has 'locked' in a certain position, and I have been unable to open my mouth properly without causing pain. Hence the term 'lock jaw'—a term which some people give to this severe manifestation of TMJ disorder.

What causes TMJ disorder?

There is probably no single cause for TMJ disorder. Arthritis, dislocation, clenching of the jaw (many people do this to relieve tension), and grinding of teeth (bruxism) have all been implicated.

In my own case, when I was a child, my parents could hear me grinding my teeth at night—even when I was as young as five years old!

Many people say that stress is a major factor in causing TMJ disorder.

Treatment for TMJ disorder

Getting a proper diagnosis

Treatment depends on ascertaining the cause in your particular case (if this can be determined). It is generally accepted that there is rarely a complete cure, and that good management of TMJ disorder is the most viable option. Surgery is rarely required.

If you experience painful symptoms, it is wise to see a cranio-maxillary (facial) surgeon or a dentist. This will involve a physical examination, and might include some X-rays—although these are often normal and it is difficult to see any abnormalities.

Some general hints on management

Because the muscles and nerves in your jaw are closely connected to those in your ear, treatment to relax all of these muscles can be effective.

Other treatments include heat packs to your face (especially in the case of muscle spasms), chewing softer foods (no crunchy refrigerated apples please), and medications that relax the muscles.

In my case, I was first sent to a physiotherapist for weekly massages to my upper back and neck area. I was also given exercises to relieve stress in my face, tongue, jaw, and neck. I also found that using the Alexander technique was extremely beneficial in correcting posture and fixing the balance of my upper body.

Mouth guards

Later I went to a surgeon, and then to a dentist who specialised in TMJ disorder. A mouth guard was fitted, to be worn when sleeping. This prevents me from grinding my teeth at night, and also realigns my jaw to sit in the right position. It was a little uncomfortable at first, but now I suffer pain only if I don't wear it on a frequent basis. I probably use it two or three times a week, and I find that it alleviates the problem. The mouth guard can be a little drying on the throat (because it leaves my mouth slightly open) so I don't use it every night. As I say, two or three times a week is enough to control the pain.

I have also noticed that the problem increases when I am on tour. I believe it is because I am sleeping in a different bed every night and sitting in a tour bus for hours on end—combined with the added pressures of being on the road. So I make sure I take my mouth guard with me, do my exercises and stretches, and stay relaxed. (And I do get used to the crew making jokes about it!)

Tinnitus
What is it?
The term 'tinnitus' comes from a Latin word meaning 'to tinkle or ring a bell'. Those who suffer from it experience a perception of ringing in the ears—or perhaps hissing, roaring, clicking, chirping, or whistling sounds. These sounds are heard only by the sufferer. They can be constant or intermittent; soft or loud.

I know many musicians and singers who experience tinnitus. It is disrupting not only in performing, but also in every area of their lives. However, it can be reduced and sometimes it can be cured. More importantly, it can be prevented all together.

The causes of tinnitus
There are several causes of tinnitus. The best known is exposure to loud noise—which is why it is quite a common complaint of those in the music and entertainment industries.

Other causes include:

- a build-up of wax in the air canal;
- ear and sinus infections;
- jaw misalignment (TMJ disorder); and
- certain medications (including aspirin taken in large doses).

Stress, fatigue, caffeine, nicotine, and alcohol can all worsen the effects of tinnitus. So can certain foods and drinks with high sugar, salt, and fat content—such as wine, cheese, and chocolate.

What should I do about it?

If you think that you have tinnitus, the first thing you should do is see an ear, nose and throat specialist to get a correct diagnosis. You might well be advised to have a hearing test.

The doctor will be able to determine whether the cause is a medical condition (such as a sinus infection) or environmental damage (such as exposure to loud noise). Treatment can then be tailored accordingly.

Some treatments for tinnitus

Cure is rare. The most frequent cause is nerve damage in your ear—which is irreparable. However, here is a brief overview of some of the treatments available to alleviate (and possibly cure) tinnitus.

Hearing aids

Hearing aids often reduce tinnitus because they amplify a lot of noise in the 'outside world'—thus drowning out the ringing sensation in the ears. This does not always work, but some sufferers have had success with this method.

Masking

The term 'masking' refers to the patient wearing a similar device to that of a hearing aid. This device is fitted with low-level noise, which is set at a very low level so it does not affect normal hearing. After a while this sound cannot even be heard unless the patient really tries to hear it. The aim of masking is to help the brain ignore the tinnitus signals.

Drugs

Anti-anxiety drugs (such as Xanax), some anti-depressants, anti-histamines, anti-convulsants, and some anaesthetics have been known to reduce the severity of tinnitus. Obviously there are side-effects to taking medications, and these should be discussed with your specialist.

Bio-feedback

Bio-feedback is a relaxation technique used to control specific bodily functions such as heart rate, brainwave activity, and muscle tension. It works by changing the body's reaction to stress. This, in turn, can reduce the severity of tinnitus in some people.

Natural therapies
Magnesium, zinc, ginkgo, biloba, homoeopathic remedies, and B vitamins have all been useful for some sufferers.

How can I avoid tinnitus?
Specialists agree that the most effective way to avoid tinnitus is to avoid noise levels above 90dB over an 8-hour period. Invest in some professional musicians' earplugs to wear when you are performing, and have a hearing test every 12 to 18 months if you believe you are at risk.

Among other causes of tinnitus, some circumstances (such as a sinus or ear infection) can often not be avoided. But do your best to avoid becoming run down or stressed.

Dry mouth
Causes
A dry mouth can be caused by anxiety and nervousness. It can also arise as a result of the conditions in your working environment. Smoky rooms or air-conditioning can be cause problems. Even open-air concerts cause problems in some people.

These conditions often lead to a decrease in the secretion of the saliva which lubricates the mouth and throat.

What can I do?
Drinking water, sucking a slice of lemon (especially good if working in dry environments), or smelling vinegar should all promote saliva secretion.

If you suffer from a dry mouth persistently, try the mixture described in the box (page 159). This mixture moistens a dry mouth and throat. It is safe if swallowed, soothes your vocal apparatus, and has anti-bacterial properties.

> **Dry mouth mixture**
>
> **Ingredients**
> - 30 mL glycerin;
> - 10 mL aloe vera juice; and
> - 10 mL honey.
>
> **Method**
> 1. Place all of the ingredients in a small spray bottle.
> 2. Shake well before use.
> 3. Spray into your mouth when needed.

Using an unnatural voice
What does this mean?

Apart from the various medical conditions noted above in this chapter, working singers can suffer problems simply by using an unnatural voice—that is by not using your natural singing or speaking voice. What I mean by this is singing out of your range, mimicking character voices, or speaking too low or too high.

It is interesting that many performers have as much problem with their speaking voice as they do with their singing voice. To produce a very low-pitched speaking voice (which is extremely common in singers) actually takes much more work and muscle tension, and shows a lack of correct breathing. You might think that it's easier to speak in this range on the morning after the big gig—but you are actually making it harder on yourself in the long run.

Other performers take on roles that require them to imitate a certain type of voice—as in a musical or stage show. It has been proven that laryngeal muscle tension increases in this scenario. The singer might be asked to sing out of his or her range, or tighten and close the throat to create a certain quality of sound.

Some things to watch out for

Apart from what we have already mentioned in this chapter for vocal maintenance, here are some other things to keep in mind.

- Make sure that you do nothing that causes pain or hoarseness—such as yelling, screaming, or singing too loudly. Use good breathing, especially if you are doing character voices.

- Pay close attention to your speaking voice. If I am very tired, I try not to speak 'in my boots' because I know from past experience that it makes my voice more tired. I make a conscious effort to lift my voice above the 'croaky breathy' sound. This requires a little work at first—but you will be surprised at how your voice will respond.

Chapter 15

You are what you eat

Chapter 15
You are what you eat

Eating well on tour is not easy

Trying to eat well on tour is not easy, even at the best of times. I remember being on tour in New Zealand with ten guys and one other girl. We had to stop at fast food places at least every day! Once we had fast food three times in 24 hours—breakfast, lunch, and dinner. I contracted food poisoning on that tour. I'm not saying it was from the fast food—but I don't think I saw one vegetable on that tour, unless it was in a magazine!

Your energy requirements on tour are many and varied, and are often quite high. All entertainers must be aware of this as they must meet the practical demands of energy that a tour requires. But this does not mean eating high-calorie, non-nutritious foods—in fact, quite the contrary.

Glycaemic food management

I follow a program of glycaemic food management prepared by my nutritionist, Terry Martinesz. This is a nutritional program based on keeping energy levels stable and consistent throughout the day. Such a program suits most people on tour.

Glycaemic food management involves having lots of fresh fruits and vegetables, drinking lots of water, and having foods that sustain you with energy—as opposed to foods that drain you of energy. What we are really talking about is the desirability of unprocessed foods as opposed to processed foods.

Most of the foods recommended by Terry are of an unprocessed nature. This includes fruits such as apples, pears, strawberries, nectarines, peaches, plums, and so on. It is best to choose fresh fruits in season. Lots of fresh vegetables are also a good idea—including broccoli, Brussels sprouts, and cauliflower. Meats such as fish or chicken are good as a protein source.

The trick is to eat these foods regularly and evenly throughout the day—thus sustaining energy levels. Because a lot of take-away foods are highly processed, they are deficient in many quality nutrients, and are not a good choice for busy travelling singers. They are certainly practical and convenient, but they don't have the nourishment that we need to fulfil our nutritional requirements.

Quick guide to good food choices

Here is a list of food choices that will keep your body and mind well fuelled.

Fruits

Apples, oranges, strawberries, kiwi fruit, grapefruit, pears, mandarins, apricots, nectarines, peaches, plums, cherries, and grapes are all nutritious and healthy.

Juices

Fresh juice first thing in the morning is a great way to start the day. This can be expensive and difficult, but if you find a place that offers fresh juices make the most of it! A good choice is apple, celery, and ginger juice, or celery and beetroot juice. To minimise sugar levels and to maximise vitamin and mineral absorption, it is preferable to consume vegetable juices rather than pure fruit juices. Cucumber, carrot, and tomato juices are all good choices.

Vegetables

Avocado, tomatoes, capsicum, snow peas, mushrooms, lettuce, celery, onion, carrot, broccoli, cabbage, asparagus, and cucumber are all good.

Yoghurt

'Live' yoghurt can be found in most supermarkets and is the best yoghurt to eat as a source of beneficial bacteria. Any yoghurt that contains live bacteria (sounds lovely, doesn't it?) and low sugar is fine.

Nuts

Raw unsalted almonds are very nutritious.

Meat

Deep ocean fish, tuna, salmon, chicken, and topside steak (or stir-fry strips) are all good sources of protein.

Soups

I recommend courgette, cauliflower, and vegetable soups.

How to implement good diet practices

Being away from home means that the foods to which you are accustomed might not always be available. This is especially true when travelling overseas.

Dietary modification is unavoidable at times, and it is therefore acceptable in the short term to make the best choices you can with what you have. You should generally be able to find something suitable from the food options listed below:

Breakfast

- celery, apple and ginger juice, a couple of pieces of low glycaemic index (low GI) fruit;
- a bowl of fruit and yoghurt, with a sprinkling of raw unsalted almonds;
- porridge with hot water and a sprinkling of dried fruit;
- canned low-fat rice pudding;
- dry cereal (for example, low-fat and low-sugar muesli or bran flakes) with skimmed milk and sultanas.

Lunch

- tuna, salmon, or avocado salad;
- low-fat and low-salt soup (for example, canned or light 'cuppa soup' varieties);
- low-salt baked beans and rice cakes;
- rice cakes with tuna, canned salmon, or avocado;
- healthy breads.

Dinner

- grilled fish with vegetables or salad;
- beef, chicken, or vegetable stir fries;
- gluten-free pasta (if you can get it) with a tomato-based sauce;
- boiled rice with canned tuna or salmon and tomato-based sauce;
- rice salad with canned corn, peas, carrots, asparagus, and Lima beans;
- instant noodles (low-fat varieties);
- frozen vegetables.

Snacks

- raw unsalted almonds;
- low GI fruit or vegetables;
- healthy low-fat bars (for example, muesli, soy, sesame, or nut);
- dried fruit;
- protein shakes (available from health food shops).

Fluid intake

- remember to drink lots of water—about two litres a day;
- herbal teas—stay away from tea and coffee if you can because they can have a dehydrating effect.

Eating and performing

How much (and when) you eat really depends on the energy expenditure of your performance. For example, a Broadway show singer or dancer exerts more energy than someone playing the piano and singing for an evening. A three-hour concert obviously requires more energy than a 45-minute set.

I find that most performers (including myself) are not very hungry before a performance—and starving afterwards! This is often due to the excitement and nerves of performing. (To all you singers who never get nervous—all I can say is that I'm jealous...) Some people find it difficult to sing on a full stomach. Being Italian, I never have that problem!

I often plan my day around when I will be singing. If I have a 7 pm gig, I usually have plenty of snacks throughout the day, an early dinner (say at 5 pm), and another snack after the performance at about 10 pm. Make sure you eat something before you sing—you don't want to be feeling ill or tired during your performance. This has happened to me several times, and on one occasion I fainted—not a pleasant thing to do in front of people!

If your performance is quite rigorous, a special glucose polymer formula during your performance is a great idea. An easily purchased commercial product is Lucozade. There are other products, but a nutritionist should be consulted to formulate one that specially suits your needs.

Liquids

Make sure you drink lots of water throughout the day and during your performance. Ice-cold drinks are not advisable during a performance because they can constrict your vocal folds and therefore create tension. If you have warmed-up your voice to perform, very cold drinks can be a shock to your system. Tap water or lukewarm drinks are the best choice.

If you have a sore throat and still need to sing, mix some honey and lemon with your water to sip throughout the night. If it hurts to swallow, cancel the engagement—this means that your vocal folds are inflamed and that singing can cause damage.

Some final thoughts

Most healthy foods are significantly more expensive than fast food. My advice is to stop at a supermarket and stock up.

When you do stop somewhere to eat a meal, ask for what you want. If all you want is grilled chicken and vegetables, most restaurants are happy to oblige—even if it's not on the menu.

Of course, it's not easy to get it right every time, and sometimes all you want is a good hearty meal and a glass of wine! The occasional treat is fine. But if you are eating like that all the time you will be fighting against your body instead of working with it.

Enjoy yourself and your job, and implement the right food choices as much as you can.

Peace, love, and mung beans!

Chapter 16

What to do with a tired voice

Chapter 16
What to do with a tired voice

Hints to avoid vocal fatigue

As a singer, you will inevitably experience some vocal fatigue. When you are exhausted and working hard, your body becomes tired and does not support your voice sufficiently. But if you sang only when your voice was in peak condition, you might sing only a couple of times a year!

When you become tired, it is easy to fall into bad habits because you feel under tension to perform at peak level in difficult circumstances. Here are a few tips to help you when you find yourself in this situation.

Drink lots of water

Drinks lots of water to rehydrate your throat and keep your vocal folds moist.

Avoid caffeine

Avoid any beverages that contain caffeine because they dry your throat, and thus exacerbate vocal fatigue and tension.

Avoid antihistamines

If you are going to sing for long periods of time, stay away from antihistamines or other medications that dry up mucus. Antihistamines are excellent for easing congestion and irritation, but they do have a drying effect on your vocal folds. Well-lubricated vocal folds are important for efficient singing.

Huge doses of vitamin C in conjunction with antihistamine tablets can also have a drying effect.

Be careful with throat gargles and cough sweets

Throat gargles and cough lollies with menthol will dry out your throat. Those with anaesthetic are also a risk because you will not know how much damage you are doing. These medications can hide infection, strain, and tension.

Vocal warm-up and warm-down

If you have a tired voice, but still need to fulfil singing commitments, do a light vocal warm-up first thing in the morning. This will help you to speak and sing with correct placement throughout the day.

If you save your warm up for the afternoon, or just before your gig, you might find that your voice is tired from incorrect placement during the day. A warm-up of about an hour in the morning is great, followed by a warm-up before your performance in the evening.

To warm down, you can use the same vocal exercises you use to warm up.

Avoid aspirin

It is important to stay away from aspirin if you are doing a lot of singing. Aspirin is an anticoagulant, which means it thins the blood. This can weaken your vocal membranes and can trigger bleeding or damage.

Instead of aspirin, you can take paracetamol. Talk to your health professional about other options.

Don't cough or clear your throat

Never clear your throat or cough voluntarily to get rid of mucus. This will increase vocal fatigue. When you clear your throat, you actually aggravate your vocal folds. This causes more mucus to be secreted to rectify the problem, and this then becomes a continuous cycle.

The best thing to do to shift mucus is to drink water, swallow, or 'sing it off' your folds. (That is, after you have warmed-up, do some arpeggios or scales which slide quickly up and down your register.)

Sleep

This is just commonsense—if you are tired, get some sleep! Get as much sleep as you can! Try not to sleep too close to your performance time. This is unusual anyway because nerves set in—but some people can do it!. Sleeping too close to your performance can leave you feeling groggy, and it can take longer to get your voice to wake up with you!

Avoid smoking and smoky environments

Stay away from smoke and smoke-filled rooms. These can have a dehydrating effect.

Look after your speaking voice

Concentrate on your speaking voice. Many singers think that they are resting their voices for a gig in the evening if, during the day, they whisper or keep their voices low and 'breathy'. This is actually more tiring for your voice and will make it worse.

Support your speaking voice as you would support your singing voice. Don't speak too high or too low, but keep your voice resonant and forward—try to speak above the 'croak'. Use your breath to support your speaking voice as you would your singing voice.

Vocal rest

Complete vocal rest is very beneficial

Complete vocal rest can be good if your voice is extremely tired. But this is often difficult for working singers. You and your doctor need to assess how tired your voice really is. Vocal rest is a last resort when your voice is not responding to anything else.

There are many singers who rarely rest their voices. Their voices are in a constant state of tiredness. If your voice is exhausted, you will find that a few days to a week of no singing and speaking can do amazing things for your voice. However, keep in mind that complete vocal rest is of no use at all if the reason for the original problem is bad technique. Rest will help, but as soon as you start singing again, you will fall into your same old habits—which will result in fatigue all over again. My suggestion is to get some lessons—and read this book!

And remember not to whisper during a state of vocal rest—this is more tiring than speaking. Read a book, watch a movie, write a letter—and put the answering machine on!

After a period of vocal rest, remember to be gentle with your voice. The longer you rest, the longer it will take for your voice to be back to its peak level. For example, don't rest for two weeks and then start singing immediately on the afternoon of a big vocal performance. You will do more harm than good. My suggestion in a case like this is to start warming-up your voice a few days to a week before your performance—depending on how much time you have, and how much time you've rested.

Avoid singing when physically tired

If you are physically exhausted, think twice about singing. No matter how experienced you are as a vocalist, it is hard to put good technique into practice when you are physically tired. If possible, do not sing under these conditions. You will do more harm than good.

Yawning and massaging your throat

Yawning does to your throat what a good stretch does for your body! It's great for relaxing your throat. This is especially true when tension is evident.

I also find that massaging my throat, jaw, and neck helps to relieve tension.

Chapter 17
Stage fright

Chapter 17
Stage fright

The 'No. 1 fear' of most people

Apparently the 'No. 1 fear' that people have is speaking in public. The 'No. 2 fear' is death. According to Jerry Seinfeld, that means that more people at a funeral would rather be in the casket than giving the eulogy!

Performance anxiety ('stage fright') is likely to occur whenever you are presenting something that is important to you and to other people. The core of stage fright is thinking about the possible things that can go wrong when you are on stage.

Signs and symptoms

Some of the signs and symptoms of stage fright include trembling, dry throat, sudden tiredness, nausea, difficulty concentrating, shortness of breath, lack of vocal control, exaggerated fear, anxiety attacks, lack of coordination, a feeling of impending faintness, emotional flatness, and an inability to see or hear correctly.

Most performers have probably experienced one or more of these signs and symptoms at some time. Indeed, some people say that it is good to feel a little nervous because it keeps you on your toes. However, the balance between having stage 'presence' and coping with the 'jitters' is very difficult for people who have severe stage fright.

Is it normal?

If you have experienced stage fright or performance anxiety, you are not alone. One of the most important things that will help you to overcome your fear is to realise that you are not alone.

The more creative you are, the more likely you are to experience stage fright. Fear is the greatest crippler of talent and your true self, but you can overcome it. I have experienced severe stage fright during the course of my career so I know what I am talking about! You are not alone, and you don't have to find another line of work.

Causes and management

Often the cause of performance anxiety is a negative thought pattern. It is therefore important to address what is happening in your mind, and then try to do something about the nervous reaction in your body.

Here are a few tips that have been used quite successfully by me and by others. But don't be afraid to consult a professional or undertake some helpful courses. You will find professional assistance and courses to be very beneficial. And remember that you are normal!

Think about the root of your fear

The first thing you should do is sit down and think about the root of your fear. You have more chance of coping with nervousness if you understand what it is that makes you nervous.

- Is it because you don't feel confident in your appearance?
- Do you feel overweight or underweight?
- Do you feel that your voice needs work?
- Are you afraid you won't do a good job?
- Did something happen in the past that triggered your fear?

Talk to someone about it and think of ways to overcome it. One of the worst things you can do is ignore your problem. Stare fear right in the face!

Imagine

I have found that positive 'day-dreaming' has been one of the best things I can do for overcoming performance anxiety. Imagine your performance, and in that day dream imagine that you are unbelievably confident. Look at yourself—you are well dressed, calm, singing and performing well, and the audience is responding positively. But most of all, you are having the time of your life!

I remember my first television performance. I was so nervous that I thought I was going to pass out. I determined that the next time I did live television I was not going to feel like that. When the next engagement came up, I imagined how well I would do and how much fun I would have. I proposed to do this every day until the actual performance day—which was about eight weeks away. And you know what? It was an amazing time! I have fond memories of how much fun I had.

The funny thing about this particular performance was that something actually went wrong on live television—and we all handled it really well! It did not phase any of us!

So go over the top with your day dreaming.

Self talk

There is an old proverb that says: 'Death and life are in the power of the tongue'. And there is scientific evidence that this sentiment is basically right! Experiments have been done on the power which the words you speak can have on your body. They discovered that different words released different hormones—and made the body react accordingly. They found that people who spoke positively were healthier and less stressed!

So start talking to yourself! This is a good way to get rid of deep-seated negative attitudes. Look in the mirror and tell yourself that you are good at what you do. It's not pretentious to have a good self-image. I often tell myself: 'You can do this Roma, you have something good to give to the world'; or 'You are going to do a great job tonight Roma; you are confident and you can make a difference in people's lives!'

You might feel silly but it's amazing what it does to your spirit.

Be yourself

Be authentic. People love it when you are honest, and when they know that they are getting the 'real' person during a performance. Be who you are, not whom you think people would like you to be.

You don't have to be something that you are not—I don't care what any record company executive says! Remember you *are* special. There is no one else like you in the whole world—so you *do* have something of value to give by just being yourself.

Give yourself permission to feel

Don't be afraid to be moved by the music, or by the event. Lots of people who experience anxiety go to the opposite extreme and become emotionally unresponsive. In this way, they hope that they can cope when they perform.

In the long term, this approach doesn't work. You will disconnect from the audience, and you won't enjoy yourself like you should.

Allow yourself to feel excited, nervous, or moved by a particular piece.

One of the biggest breakthroughs I have had was on a particular night when I had a panic attack in the middle of a performance. I was so sick of being nervous all the time that I said to myself: 'Oh well, what's the worst that can happen? I pass out and then I wake up, and I'm still alive. I am doing what I love. And, at the end of the day, the most important thing is not this stage— it's my family and my friends; it's caring about people; it's why I wrote these songs. The most important thing is that I actually got to write these songs, and that I expressed myself to my friends and colleagues.' It was a wonderful feeling to have that revelation and to be at peace to enjoy the rest of the night!

Be a giver not a taker

Instead of thinking about how the audience will respond, concentrate on what you can give them to take home. Wouldn't it be awesome if, years later, people remembered something you said or sang because it left an impact? Take the focus off yourself.

Some practical tips
Concentrate on what you are singing or saying
One of the best ways to overcome stage fright is to concentrate on what you are singing or playing. Think about the words, the feelings, and the images—and how you can communicate these things with the audience. Do this during rehearsals, and do it during the performance.

Be prepared
Make sure that you practise. This way there is less of a chance of things going wrong.

Dress for success
If you feel good about they way you look, you will feel more confident that you can give a good performance.

If you are a girl, treat yourself to getting your hair and your nails done. (Then again, I shouldn't be sexist—perhaps guys could do this too!)

Exercise
Being active as part of your daily regime actually works wonders. You feel good about yourself. Exercise releases 'feel-good' endorphins throughout your body, and these make you feel more confident and in charge.

Isometrics and stretching
Exercises that tighten and release the muscles are excellent. By doing these exercises you use up all that adrenalin flowing around your body. This can make you feel calmer.

Breathing
Concentrate on your breathing. Take long deep breaths in and out to help release tension.

No caffeine
Caffeine is a stimulant. Avoid it. If you are a nervous performer, you don't need anything else to help raise your pulse rate!

Do some low-key performances

If you really are having trouble with stage fright, do some gigs that are not too high-profile—gigs in which there is little pressure. Work your way up to a major gig by doing work that is less stressful first. Or do backing vocals for a while until you get used to feeling more confident out front on your own.

Watch other performers and ask questions

You will be surprised at how many people struggle with stage fright. I feel so much better knowing that performers I admire also struggle with nerves. Ask lots of questions to see what they do to help them overcome their fears.

And don't forget that you can do it! Have faith in yourself.

Chapter 18

How to find
a good teacher

Chapter 18
How to find a good teacher

Not the impossible dream!

Some people think that trying to find the ideal teacher is the impossible dream! Well, the good news is that it is *not* impossible. But you do need to know what to look for if you want to avoid wasting your money.

Things to look for

From my experience these are some of the qualities which I suggest you look for in a great teacher.

Good at diagnosis

A good teacher must have the ability to diagnose correctly with a view to correcting specific functional vocal problems.

This is a very important quality—especially if you are a professional singer. Most vocal difficulties are caused by bad habits that can be rectified. You need someone who can tell when your voice is not in good shape, who can tell you exactly why it is not in good shape, and who has the expertise to help you correct any functional problems you have.

Keep in mind that you don't need to be in pain to be experiencing vocal difficulty. Sometimes it takes a discerning teacher to make you aware of what you are doing with your voice.

Persistent and strong

A good teacher must be persistent and strong with you. I love my teacher because she doesn't spend the whole lesson telling me how great I am! She gives praise when it is due, but she is firm and tells it like it is!

If you are singing professionally, you are obviously good at what you do, so you don't need a 'pat on the back' every five minutes. You don't need another fan! You need someone who won't settle for anything less than the best out of you.

You need someone who will help you reach your peak. You need someone who will make you practise (and who will not listen to your excuses when you don't!)

It is a rare person who can be firm without being mean or insulting. When you find someone like this—hold on to that person firmly!

Lets you ask questions

A good teacher lets you ask questions. If you don't understand why you are doing something, you should not feel afraid to ask questions.

Your teacher won't know everything—no one does. But a good teacher should never feel threatened by an inquisitive student. A good teacher might sometimes be slightly annoyed by questions—but never threatened!

Well rounded

A good teacher is well rounded. This doesn't mean overweight! It means that you need someone who understands all aspects of singing—not just one specific area.

Breathing, resonance, posture, and so on—there are so many aspects of singing that contribute to good vocal technique. A well-rounded teacher who has knowledge and experience in all these areas will make you a well-rounded singer.

Good musicianship skills

A good teacher should have good musicianship skills. It is obvious that a teacher who can play the piano and read music has enormous advantages over a teacher who cannot do these things! Just as any teacher needs these sorts of basic skills, a *really good* teacher has *really good* musicianship skills.

A good communicator

A good teacher must be a good communicator. Knowledge is of no use to anyone else if it can't be communicated to others.

Always learning

Good teachers are always learning themselves. A good teacher is always learning the latest information about his or her craft. These teachers are willing to improve and adapt their teaching skills according to what they have learnt.

This doesn't mean that they change the fundamentals of what they are teaching. But they are always learning new ways to improve their students' understanding of singing and techniques for doing it well.

A good teacher is always willing to incorporate new concepts that build on the foundations of what they teach.

Recommended by others

A good teacher is often highly recommended by others. This is one of the best ways to find the right teacher for you. If a teacher is good, you will hear about him or her.

However, beware of fads. Some teachers are in fashion for a season, but might not be teaching you correctly.

Allows you to record lessons

A good teacher allows you to record the lesson. I am surprised that a lot of teachers do not do this. I once had a student who had lived and worked in London and who had spent time going to a very well-known teacher there. Not only did the teacher charge an unbelievable amount of money, but the students were never allowed to tape the lessons. This was supposedly because her teaching methods were under copyright!

The best thing about recording your lesson is that you hear your teacher's corrections over and over again. This makes every private practice very beneficial.

I don't keep tapes of everything. However, if I have a particularly helpful lesson I keep it for future reference. For example, if I have a cold, Loris takes me through a different set of exercises from those she would suggest if my voice were in top condition. I keep a tape of this lesson, and whenever I have the same problems I pull out this tape and listen to it. This is very beneficial if I am on tour and I am by myself. I often take a few different tapes on tour with me to help me warm up.

Teaching you to think for yourself

A good teacher teaches you to think for yourself. As you progress through your lessons, you should be learning skills that help you make good judgments for yourself. You should have a greater understanding of good and bad technique, and rely less on your teacher for affirmation.

Once he or she has set you off in the right direction, you should be able to gain more confidence in your own abilities. You should be able to use what you have been taught.

Things to avoid

Having discussed some of the good things to look for in a teacher, here are some of the things you should seek to avoid in choosing a teacher.

'I'll make you into a star'

Beware of teachers who tell you that they can make you into a star. As I said previously, you don't need a pat on the back! You don't need another fan! You need someone who will direct and guide you in the right direction.

Insulting and degrading teachers

Beware of teachers who insult you and degrade you. This is the opposite end of the scale to the teacher who wants to be a fan! Unfortunately I know of teachers who do this sort of thing. They insult and degrade their students, and have students leaving their lessons in tears. You don't need to be bullied into singing properly.

Teachers who 'name drop'

Beware of people who are constantly telling you who they have taught. If a person is a good teacher, other singers will recommend that person.

Good teachers don't need to recommend themselves by talking about their more famous pupils. I find it disconcerting when teachers brag about singers they have taught. Singers who have a real profile prefer their privacy and it is the responsibility of the teacher to protect that privacy and treat his or her pupils with respect. If a teacher is in the habit of talking to you about someone else, you can assume that this teacher is also in the habit of talking about you to someone else! Not very professional at all!

Teachers who talk non-stop

Teachers who are too 'chatty' and talk throughout a lesson are usually professional singers themselves. They tend to treat you as a peer, rather than as a student.

Remember that you are paying good money to learn. You are not paying for a chat with a friend!

'I have, of course, invented my own technique'

Beware of teachers who tell you that they have invented their own technique. This is absolute baloney! There are only two ways to sing—the right way and the wrong way.

There are many different methods of teaching the right way, but there are always people out there trying to sell their own 'new and easier' ways of singing. Invariably you are told that this method is 'unique'. These teachers have a knack of 'putting-down' other techniques, and usually have quite strong personalities.

If they can support what they teach with factual information, and if they can prove (medically and scientifically) the physiological benefits of their methods, I will be the first to send them a bottle of champagne! But usually they can't!

Apart from the problem of credibility, the other problem with this type of teacher is that you really *don't* want someone who is teaching a 'unique' method which only this particular teacher understands. Think about it! If this teacher really is the only person in the world who understands this new-found technique, how on earth will you ever learn to stand on your own two feet? What happens if you move interstate or overseas? In effect, this sort of claim means that you must become extremely dependent on your teacher.

A good teacher should be teaching you to think for yourself. But these 'unique' teachers are only making you utterly dependent on them.

Teachers with minimum experience

Beware of teachers with a minimum of experience, knowledge, and training. Of course, it is true that experience isn't everything. There are plenty of qualified and experienced teachers who are terrible at teaching. Qualifications don't always make a good teacher. However, on the other hand, it also true to say that someone who has had one year of singing lessons isn't going to be the best teacher for you!

One thing *is* certain. As a professional singer, you need someone who knows more than you do.

I think experience is very important as a teacher. However, sometimes experience is not enough. A good teacher not only understands the foundations of singing, but also knows enough to appreciate that he or she must constantly build on those foundations. This takes years to develop. Just to give you an idea—someone who has had two or three years of vocal training is still considered a beginner in some professional circles!

Teachers who never let you make mistakes

Beware of teachers who never let you make mistakes. I remember being in a lesson with my teacher and singing a whole scale completely wrong. The teacher let me continue! By the time that I was singing the high notes, my throat was sore and my voice started to 'crack'. I looked at my teacher in shock as if to say: 'What you are teaching me is not working!'. She smiled and said to me: 'Yes, I knew that you were doing it wrong, but I wanted you to see what would happen if you kept singing in that way!'. I think I learnt more in that lesson than I did in ten other lessons put together!

A teacher needs to correct—but a good teacher also lets students work things out for themselves. Do you know why? Because you are not stupid! He or she is trying to teach you to think for yourself. If you learn this, you will know what to do when the teacher is not around.

Once you have found a good teacher

It is difficult for full-time singers to have regular singing lessons because they are travelling and working so much. If you are in this situation, my suggestion is that once you have put your voice back into good working order with a good teacher, go back regularly for 'checkups'.

How often should you go back for a 'check up'? This depends on how much training you have previously had, how much you regularly practise, and how much vocal trouble you are having. For example, nodules usually represent poor vocal technique, and if you develop these you might need a minimum of six months to a year of training to get back on track. Of course, if you are diligent, they disappear quite quickly—but then you need to continue training to strengthen and secure your new technique.

I wish I could have lessons all the time—but unfortunately I am not usually in the same place for long enough. So I keep practising on my own, and I go back to my teacher as frequently as possible. Every time I do this, I notice that I have very easily fallen into bad habits if I am not careful. I am always very grateful to Loris for putting my voice back in good working order!

If you can't go weekly, try monthly, and if that is impossible because of touring, a group of several lessons every six months is very beneficial. Usually you know when you are not comfortable or secure. Seek help before damage is done!

Chapter 19

Some common Q & A

Chapter 19
Some common Q & A

In the earlier chapters of this book I hope that I have been able to answer most of your questions. But if I have missed something, perhaps you will find answers to your questions here.

Will certain cough sweets, teas, sprays, and so on help me sing better?

The only thing that will help you to sing better is correct vocal technique and taking proper care of your voice. Certain preparations soothe irritated membranes, and help alleviate an upper respiratory tract infection (URTI), but none of these substances reaches the vocal folds, so they really only reduce pain and discomfort.

If I sing correctly will my voice ever get tired?

If you are singing correctly you voice should not get tired. However, if you are physically tired, your voice might seem to become fatigued. This is because singing requires physical energy. When your energy levels are depleted, you are more likely to become lazy with your technique. This, in turn, affects the quality of your voice.

Even the most experienced singer needs to take care to give the voice regular rest periods. Touring and gigging are tiring on the body.

Why is it harder to breathe properly when pregnant?

During pregnancy, your bones soften and move to allow more room for your baby to grow. During the last months of pregnancy, your diaphragm, ribcage, lungs, and even your heart are pushed upwards to make room—which makes it much more difficult to breathe comfortably. You can still sing—it's just a lot more work!

As a woman I notice that at certain times of the month I find it more difficult to sing than at other times, especially during my period. Why is this?
Any hormonal changes in your body—including menopause, pregnancy, and your menstrual cycle—can cause your vocal folds to thicken slightly. This is due to increased blood flow to your vocal folds. When your folds thicken, phonation can become more difficult, so it is important during these times to take extra care with your voice.

What is the uvula?
The uvula is the fleshy lobe, shaped like a tear drop, that hangs at the back of your throat. This area is technically called the *posterior* part of your soft palate.

What is falsetto?
Falsetto is the register of the male voice on top of 'head voice'. It is the register used when a male voice imitates a female voice. It is very high-pitched, and has less brilliance than head voice. The Italian masters of classical singing thought that this sound was unnatural—hence the term *falsetto* ('false voice').

What is flageolet?
Flageolet is the highest register of the female voice—higher than 'head voice'. A lot of people call this 'falsetto', but if we are to use correct terminology, the term 'falsetto' should be used to describe only the highest register of the male voice.

What is vibrato?
Vibrato is the rapid fluctuation of pitch slightly above or below the main pitch. It is a natural result of the balance of airflow and vocal fold approximation.

All voices have natural vibrato—because all sound is vibration. However, if your voice has a very strong 'straight' tone, vibrato can be enhanced through certain exercises.

What is tremolo?
Tremolo is a term used to describe a situation in which vibrato is excessive. This is also called 'shake'.

What is wobble?

Wobble is the opposite of tremolo. It occurs when vibrato is too slow and too wide. Wobble is also called 'oscillation'. Both tremolo and wobble are undesirable vocal characteristics.

Why do people sing out of tune?

Singing out of tune is usually a breathing problem. People who sing 'sharp' are usually tense and rigid in their breathing. Singing 'flat' is often due to a lack of 'connection' to the breath.

In some cases there is a lack of pitch awareness. This can be corrected with aural training.

Can anyone sing? Can anyone improve?

Of course! Anyone can sing, and anyone can improve. Although some singers are more naturally gifted than others, if you are disciplined and determined you can do anything.

Do you have to be able to read music to be a good singer?

No you don't. Although singers who can read music tend to learn more quickly, and although an understanding of music and musical terms is extremely beneficial, you can still advance vocally even if you do not read music.

Is the approach to singing different for males and females?

Different vocal categories require different vocal exercises. This should be determined by your teacher, but the principles laid out in this book can help any type and style of singer.

Apart from the obvious differences in sound, are male and female voices different?

Male and female voices are physiologically different. During puberty, a male larynx grows approximately 30% more than a female larynx. The membranous portion of the vocal fold is longer in an adult male, and the cartilaginous portion is smaller.

The larynx size between voice categories can also be different. For example, the larynx of a soprano can be a different size from that of an alto.

If I learn to sing correctly, will I have the same quality of voice when I am 60?

Yes you should. However, there are many factors involved in preserving your voice. Diet, exercise, pollution, and so on all play a part. And sometimes things are out of our control!

However, if you keep up a daily vocal routine, if you take care of your voice, and if you remain in good health, your voice will serve you well in later years.

Can I extend my vocal range?

You can extend your vocal range by regular practice. This develops greater flexibility in the laryngeal muscles. However, remember that you are 'born' with the voice you have—if you are a soprano, it is not likely you will ever be able to sing a low bass note. You can strengthen and develop the notes that you have, but practice will not give you notes that were never there in the first place!

Your aim in learning singing is to strengthen the notes that you *can* sing, so that all of your range is strong, confident, and clear.

What is 'belting' and is it OK for my voice?

Belting is a way of singing in which a mixture of 'chest voice' and 'middle voice' is used—combined with considerable diaphragmatic pressure. This type of singing is common in musical theatre in which the voice must be projected loudly to reach the audience. Belting is OK if resonance is present.

Bibliography

Bibliography

I used the following references for research in writing this book. If you wish to read further on the subjects covered, the following is a list of suggested books and websites.

Books

Here are some useful books, arranged in alphabetical order of the author.

Barlow, Wilfred 1973, *The Alexander Principle*, Gollancz, London.

Foster, Roland 1935, *Vocal Success and How to Achieve It—a practical guide to modern principles of vocal training, with graduated exercises and studies for all voices,* W. H. Paling & Co., Sydney and London.

Marchesi, Mathilde 1970, Bel Canto: *A Theoretical and Practical Vocal Method*, Dover Publications, New York.

McCallion, Michael 1998, *The Voice Book*, Faber & Faber Ltd, London.

Miller, Richard 1996, *The Structure of Singing*, Schirmer Books, USA.

Slater, David D. 1911, *Vocal Physiology and the Teaching of Singing*, J. H. Larway, London.

Websites

Here are some useful websites, arranged according to particular subjects of interest.

Alexander Technique

If you are interested in the Alexander technique, try this website.

Alexander technique

<www.synergy-health.co.uk/alexander%20technique/atbenefits.htm>, accessed March 2001.

Stage fright

If you are interested in the the subject of stage fright, try these websites.

Managing stage fright

<http://www.soapboxorations.com/squiggles/stagefright.htm>

Transform stage fright into magnetic presence

Zimmer, Sandra

<www.selfgrowth.com/articles/zimmer5.html>

Tinnitus

If you are interested in the subject of tinnitus, try this website.

American Tinnitus Association

<www.ata.org>

TMJ syndrome

If you are interested in the the subject of TMJ syndrome, try this website.

<http://www.emedicinehealth.com/articles/14227-1.asp>

Voice disorders

If you are interested in the the subject of voice disorders, try this website.

Centre for Voice Disorders of Wake Forest University

<www.bgsm.edu/voice/singers/>

What people are saying about *The Working Singer's Handbook*

It doesn't matter how long you have been working as a singer, you never stop learning and relearning things. I took this book with me on a recent hectic tour away, and read it on planes, in cars (I had to stop that, as I felt carsick!), and backstage. I reassessed my warm-up and breathing, tried some of the vocal exercises, and generally spent a lot of time looking at what I do as a singer and reflecting on what Roma has written. The book is interesting, but not intimidating, and I love the fact that it is written by a working singer, whose singing is always easy, beautiful and consistent, and not by some technician who doesn't have to practise what she preaches. I only wish that this book had been around when I started in the industry. Nonetheless, it will certainly be my handbook now—as a working singer who wants to keep learning and working on my craft as long as I'm singing. Roma has great personal and professional integrity, and I think anyone who is serious about singing will benefit from this book. I know I have!

Marina Prior

The Working Singer's Handbook is an exceptional 'one-book-says-it-all' summary of such a rich and vast, yet largely 'unsung' subject—presenting many essential techniques and practices needed to gain success in this craft. Roma's wealth of varied experience, coupled with her great communication skills, make this book engaging and extremely useful to any person, at any stage or level on his or her singing journey. Even a 'non-singer' will be curiously challenged to adopt the methods and procedures of this book, and be ultimately greatly rewarded for their efforts. Sit down and tune out, then stand up and tune in to a resource which opens ears, eyes, and mouths. You will be truly blessed!

Andrew Naylor
AMUSA
singer/songwriter, session musician
worship pastor, Christian City Church
Whitehorse, Australia

It is with great confidence that I personally endorse Roma Waterman's wonderfully informative book. The ideas expressed by the words in this book have been tried and tested over a lifetime of vocal expertise and training. As a result, I can say this is a definite 'must read' for any vocalist aspiring to reach full potential.

Darlene Zschech
worship pastor, Hillsong Church
Sydney, Australia

I have worked with Roma Waterman for several years both in live performances and in the recording studio, as well as in the area of music education. She is an exceptional vocalist with amazing technique and a heart the size of the Pacific Ocean. She is professional, dedicated, and an outstanding person to work with. Her book is the culmination of all her years of experience as a professional singer. If your dream is to sing, you should own this book. After the Bible, and your teledex, it will be the most valuable book in your collection. I thoroughly recommend it to every singer.

Jeff Crabtree
BA, Dip Ed (Macq); Adv Dip Chr Min, Bib Studies
Principal, School of Creative Arts
producer, songwriter, keyboard player, and vocalist
(Dr Bob and the Amazing Disciples of Groove & Prayerworks)